Running Wild

Samantha Alexander lives in Lincolnshire with a variety of animals and a schedule almost as busy and exciting as her plots! She writes numerous columns for newspapers and magazines, is a teenage agony aunt for Radio Leeds and in her spare time she regularly competes in show-jumping, dressage and eventing.

Other books in the
Hollywell Stables series

HOLLYWELL STABLES

Running Wild

7

Samantha Alexander

MACMILLAN
CHILDREN'S BOOKS

First published 1995 by Macmillan Children's Books

a division of Macmillan Publishers Limited
25 Eccleston Place, London SW1W 9NF
and Basingstoke

Associated companies throughout the world

ISBN 0 330 34201 0

1 3 5 7 9 8 6 4 2

A CIP catalogue record for this book is available from
the British Library

Phototypeset by Intype, London
Printed and bound in Great Britain by Mackays of Chatham PLC, Kent

Chapter One

"I'm telling you, there's a wild horse out there!" Binny Alderidge plonked herself down at our kitchen table, ready to take on the whole world. "You don't believe me, do you? You think I've lost my marbles."

For months now we'd been reading newspaper reports of a "Black Beast" roaming Bordman Moor. People had been on television talking about a panther, a leopard, a llama, even a giraffe.

"It's better than the Loch Ness Monster," said my little sister Katie. Her best friend Danny sat beside her, his eyes wide and his bottom lip quivering.

Binny Alderidge had come to us with the story of a stallion running wild on Bordman Moor. She'd seen him from her bathroom window in the middle of the night, strong, powerful, but nervous, looking for something.

"You've got to understand—" said Sarah, our stepmother.

"Are you calling me a liar?" Binny leapt up,

glaring defiantly. She was an old lady but she was tough and wiry. She was the grittiest and most strong minded person I'd ever met.

She crumpled a faded picture of a Palomino pony in her hand, her eyes bloodshot and angry. "He's got my Angel! I know it – in here." She clasped her hand to her chest. "Something's wrong, terribly wrong!"

"Mrs Alderidge," said Ross, raking a hand through his jet-black hair, "let's just say . . ."

The air hung with tension. I didn't know what he was going to say next.

"Let's just say, we believe that you believe it. And that's a start."

"She's a bit prickly, isn't she?" Trevor, our full-time groom marched into the tack room later that day, drenched with rain, carrying Oscar, our youngest cat, who was poking his nose out from under his oilskin.

We were huddled in the tack room trying to analyse the situation.

"I like her," said Katie.

"Mel?"

"I honestly don't know," I answered. I thought she was odd from the moment I saw her. She had dyed bright ginger hair which stuck up in tufts,

2

trendy tartan trousers covered in grass stains and dog hairs, and spectacles round her neck on a chain. Her birdlike eyes were piercing.

"I can just about swallow the wild horse bit, but for it to have taken her Angel?" Ross looked as bemused as the rest of us.

Angel was a Welsh Palomino mare who had disappeared without trace a year ago. I vaguely remembered seeing pictures up in the village shop and a reward being offered. Mrs Alderidge had taken out full-page adverts in the local paper, but to no avail. Wherever Angel was, nobody came forward with any information.

"Surely a horse loose on the moor would be seen by somebody?" I said, rolling up a stable bandage. If it had been any of our horses they'd have been round people's gardens in a jiffy – they loved human company.

"Not if it's wild, it wouldn't," Trevor said.

"But this isn't the Dark Ages, there are no wild horses, not on Bordman Moor anyway."

"Maybe it's a unicorn?" said Katie.

"Oh, get real, Katie." Ross threw a sponge at her which bounced off the saddle rack. "Next thing you'll be saying that Angel was taken by aliens."

"Maybe it came from the New Forest?"

"What?"

"The stallion."

3

"Look, this isn't going to get us anywhere." Ross was exasperated. "Wherever Angel is, she's not on Bordman Moor and she's certainly not with this mystery stallion. If you ask me, it's all in Binny Alderidge's imagination."

Even so, I shivered to think of an old pony out on the moors in all this rain. Ever since we had come back from Downing Street, it had poured down in steady, persistent sheets. Purple clouds banked up against each other, water spattered out of the gutters, the drains gurgled. It didn't seem like the middle of July.

"Eh up, what's this?" Trevor peered through the drizzle-misted window across the yard to where Sarah was plodding towards us with her head held down, not even bothering to protect herself from the rain.

"I need to have a word with Danny." She stood in the doorway, sopping wet, her red hair pushed back and her eyes glistening with tears.

Danny followed her out, looking confused and anxious, and the rest of us were left to wonder what had happened.

She came back a few minutes later and told us that Danny's mother was moving to Brighton and that Danny was going with her.

We were all taken aback. Danny's huge dark eyes seemed magnified and he looked terrified, as if he'd done something wrong. Danny had been at Hollywell Stables right from the very beginning. He'd led us to Queenie who'd been suffocating and starving to death in a scrap-yard, with wire caught round her neck, and no water or food. He was part of the team.

"I'm not going, I'm not, I'm not!" Danny buried his head in Queenie's neck.

"You can come back for holidays." It sounded so pathetic, I could have kicked myself.

"How is he?" Trevor whispered over the stable door. He came in and placed his hand on Danny's shoulder.

Why did life have to be so cruel? This was Danny's home, this was where he belonged, not with a woman who suddenly decided she wanted to play mother.

Blake came in after a long hack on Colorado looking deadly serious. "I've just heard," he said. Blake was my closest friend and confidant.

"It's just not fair," I said. "Blake, it's not fair!"

I was gritting my teeth so hard it made my jaw hurt. He folded me up in his arms and my eyes started stinging. There was nothing we could do.

"Life's not fair." Trevor clanked down some

water buckets and switched on the outside tap full blast.

"She's coming tomorrow morning," Ross said.

When Danny first came to live at Hollywell he'd had a carrier bag of belongings. It was pathetic and pitiful and Sarah had been moved to tears. Since then we'd watched him blossom with confidence and happiness. He'd gone to school every day with Katie and he was even losing his stutter and learning to read properly.

"Mel, you've got to accept it. When all's said and done, she's still his mother." Blake lifted Colorado's show-jumping saddle on to the top of the door and tickled me under the chin. How was it he always knew how to make me feel better?

Danny was far calmer after having a long talk to Trevor and by the time we'd finished lunch and watched an Australian soap he was even smiling.

Chapter Two

Mrs Mac, our chief fund raiser and secretary, telephoned later to say she'd call round that afternoon and what about a welly-wanging competition, whatever that was, or a Donkey Derby?

"She's panicking," said Sarah, writing down an idea for her latest novel on the back of the electricity bill. "I can just tell, she even called me Sandra."

In ten days we were holding the very first Hollywell Stables Gala Open Day and although none of us would admit it, we were all terrified. We'd tried to gauge how many people would be coming by putting a form in the last newsletter, but it all seemed to be getting out of control. There was so much to organize: craft stalls, burger bars, cream teas, entertainment, car parks to rope off and where to put the portable loos. Sarah was decidedly fraught and the paddocks were just one great muddy swamp. To top it all, our famous patron, Rocky, had gone on a safari in Africa and couldn't be traced.

"Are you sure you told him it was July and not September?" Sarah said, looking pointedly at me as I tried to slope off to find Blake.

It was always difficult getting through to Rocky because he had such an entourage of bodyguards and personal managers. When I'd last spoken to him he'd just come off stage after performing in Los Angeles for the President of the United States. His voice was hoarse, and he said he could barely hear me after all the noise of the concert. His ears were ringing. What if I had got it wrong? It didn't bear thinking about.

Ross suggested scrubbing up the last of the winter rugs and surcingles and I dived out of the kitchen. Jigsaw was sprawled on the only dry bit of concrete in the yard, and Walter our wayward mule had let himself out of the stable and was devouring one of Sarah's hanging baskets.

"This is the life." Katie perched on the edge of the water trough. The rain had stopped, which was a miracle, and a huge rainbow stretched from our fields right over to the other side of the village.

"Aren't they supposed to be lucky?" Danny asked.

"Only if you want a pot of gold," said Katie.

"I just want one wish," Danny sighed.

A lime-green Mini Metro shot up the drive like a rally car and Binny Alderidge got out.

"You wanted proof," she said. "Well, I've got it." She slammed a brown file down on top of the wheelbarrow.

"Aye, aye," Trevor whispered as Binny Alderidge braced herself in front of Ross as if he were the sworn enemy.

A pack of small dogs yapped non-stop inside the Mini Metro and Jigsaw looked completely unnerved and tried to blend into the stable block.

"Let's go inside," suggested Ross, and we all followed him.

"So you see, it is possible," said Binny, showing us a newspaper cutting. It was dated a few months back and the headline read: WILD PONIES FOUND ON MARSH. It told the story of four ponies which had been discovered living wild on a marshland. They were in terrible condition and one had to be put down. The only rational answer was that they'd been dumped.

"I can't believe we haven't heard about this." Sarah didn't know what to say.

"It only made local news." Binny twiddled her spectacles. "I only saw it because I was visiting my sister."

"Listen to this," I said, reading aloud. " 'People are thought to be increasingly turning horses loose as soon as the novelty wears off. Just like people dumping puppies, they want to get rid of the responsibility and have no thought for the consequences.' "

"This is serious," said Ross as he reread the article.

"That stallion has been dumped – I would bet on it!" said Binny.

Cogs slowly began to click into gear in my head. Stallions were the hardest horses to look after. They were a common victim of neglect; it all started to add up.

"This is one of the worst things I've ever heard of," said Sarah, flopping back into the armchair with Jigsaw. "It's terrible – how can someone do that?"

"Just like they can dump cats and dogs," said Trevor. "There are some really cruel people out there."

"And there's more," added Binny, her face softer now that we were listening, now that someone was taking notice.

"Here's the first sighting of the Black Beast." She passed us another newspaper cutting. "And here's when Angel went missing, just two weeks later. That's got to be more than coincidence."

"How exactly did she escape?" Sarah asked.

"The fence was smashed to smithereens. The police said it was obvious she'd been stolen – there was a professional gang going round at that time so they put two and two together."

"But you never believed them?"

"Not really. I've always had a feeling that she was alive and very close by. In the same way that I now have a feeling she's in trouble."

"I see."

"Were there any hoofprints?" Katie was using her detective brain.

"It was raining all night. If there were they'd been washed away hours before. It was just rotten luck."

Poor Binny. I was beginning to see why she'd been so desperate when she'd first visited us. For a year nobody had believed her about the Black Beast; they thought she was a dotty old lady. She'd turned to us as a last resort and we still hadn't taken any notice.

"I've got to get her back," she said. "She belonged to my husband. She's all I've got left, since he died two years ago."

Sarah put the kettle on and Katie fetched the biscuit tin. Blake came in from sorting out Colorado and Binny joked about how many handsome young men there were at Hollywell Stables. Trevor preened and Ross just went scarlet. Katie said she ought to see James, Sarah's fiancé, he could have his very own television programme. James was our

11

local vet and spent much of his time at Hollywell Stables.

"My Frank was a head-turner in his time, a real Rhett Butler."

"OK, down to business." Sarah dropped sugar lumps in everyone's tea. Katie now insisted we use lumps instead of granules so we could give them to the horses.

"Bordman Moor covers hundreds of miles. It's desolate and it's easy to get lost. Anybody could hide out up there. It's like a wilderness."

"So what you're saying is we haven't got a hope," said Ross.

"Let's just listen, shall we?" Binny winked at him and reached for a coffee cream.

"It's no good us trying to find them," Sarah paced up and down the kitchen. "Somehow we've got to get the stallion to come to us."

"But that's what I've been trying to tell you. He came looking for me last night. He stood at the edge of the paddock for a full half an hour. Something's wrong – it can only be Angel."

"How big is he?" Katie asked.

"Oh, I'd say fifteen hands, no more. An Anglo Arab."

My heart flipped with excitement. We hadn't rescued an Arab before.

"But he's wild," Binny added, "as wild as the wind, and that means dangerous."

"OK, so we'll stay at your place tonight, we'll have to stake out. James isn't working tonight, and we might need a tranquillizer gun." Sarah's mind was racing.

"Anybody good with a lasso?" Trevor asked.

"He came at midnight last night," Binny said. "But we'll have to be ready earlier, just in case."

"What if we don't catch him?" Katie asked.

"We don't want to catch him," Binny said. "We want him to take us to Angel."

"And if he doesn't?"

"He will, I know he will."

I honestly wished I had Binny's faith, but it all sounded so over the top. Blake caught my eye and I knew he was thinking the same thing.

"To tonight, then," Binny raised her mug of tea, "and I promise you won't be disappointed!"

Chapter Three

"Well, that was a waste of time," Ross said as soon as we were out of earshot.

Binny kept saying that she couldn't understand it.

"So you'll give us a ring?" Sarah opened the car door. "As soon as you see something?"

Binny lived in a pretty cottage right on the edge of Bordman Moor. The views were fantastic. We'd stayed up all night, taking it in turns to watch, but nothing had happened. Wherever the stallion was he didn't come to the cottage that night.

"Do you think she's all right?" Blake whispered as we climbed into the car.

"I think she's lonely," I said, "and this business with Angel is tearing her apart."

The disappointment was etched all over Binny's face. She seemed to have aged ten years.

"I feel such a fool," she'd said when dawn broke and there still wasn't a sign.

The cottage was full of photographs and portraits of Angel, some showing her being driven by

Binny's husband, some just loose in the paddock. There was one of Binny feeding her a carrot with Frank in the background.

"I'm worried about her," Blake said. "She's clinging to the past."

"Naah, she's a tough old bird." Trevor threw a sweet wrapper through the window and Sarah gave him a lecture on littering the countryside.

"Sorry, Mrs F."

I slapped his wrist and Blake looked at his watch. It was just after 9 a.m. We'd be home by 10. There were no prizes for guessing what we were all thinking. Danny's mother would be on the doorstep at 11 o'clock. After that we might not see him for months, if ever again. Brighton was a very long way away.

"Poor little shrimp," said Trevor.

"Blood's thicker than water," said Sarah.

Not in my book it wasn't.

We'd left Danny and Katie with Mrs Mac. The last thing we wanted was for Mrs Barrat to hear that Danny had been up all night on a wild goose chase.

Danny was with Queenie when we arrived at Hollywell. Mrs Mac had made a leaving cake and Katie had strung up some balloons and streamers.

"How is he?" Sarah asked, dumping down a pile of sleeping bags.

Mrs Mac just shook her head and turned away, choked with tears. Danny meant the world to Mrs Mac, and she'd taken him under her wing as if he were her son.

"Blake's with him now," Sarah said. "Maybe he can find the right words."

We all tried to pretend everything was all right, that nothing awful was happening. The only good thing was that the rain stopped. These last few weeks it had been like living in a monsoon.

"Put your false smiles on, everybody." Sarah glanced through the window. "Danny's mother has just arrived."

The reason we didn't trust Mrs Barrat was because she didn't show any affection for Danny. When he'd first arrived on our doorstep he was living by himself while she was staying with her boyfriend. He was nine years old and his arms and legs were like sticks. I don't think he'd ever known what it was like to sit down to a home-cooked family meal.

"Here she comes, brace yourselves," Sarah hissed.

The sharp rap at the front door was immediately answered by Trevor, who hadn't yet had the pleasure of meeting Mrs Barrat. He stood at the door blinking with shock, and I must admit I could see why.

Last time we'd seen her she'd looked like something the cat had dragged in; now she was dressed in a shell-pink summer dress and jacket and her hair was all coiffed up in an elegant style. The false eyelashes and dangly ear-rings were gone in place of a more sophisticated look.

"Fine feathers don't make fine people." Mrs Mac was not taken in.

"Earl Grey tea if you don't mind, Sarah," she said.

"What's wrong with her voice?" Trevor whispered. "She sounds terribly posh."

"More like she's read a manual on how to talk properly," I giggled, rooting through the cupboards for the tea.

"I say, this is rather nice." Mrs Barrat's husband dithered in the background. He was about twice her age and totally under her thumb. What was someone like him doing with someone like her?

"Of course, we've got the company car now." Her voice was beginning to grate on my nerves.

Mrs Mac grudgingly cut her a piece of Danny's leaving cake and Trevor searched for a clean plate. Within seconds she'd wolfed down two pieces.

Sarah's jaw was set so rigid she could barely speak and I thought she was going to explode when Mrs Barrat said she was planning on becoming a novelist, as if it was the easiest thing in the world to do.

"You could fit everything she's got to say on the back of a matchbox," Mrs Mac hissed from the walk-in pantry. "Have you noticed she's not even asked about Danny yet?"

I tried to keep a straight face and then Sarah suggested they find Danny – I don't think she could stand being cooped up with her any longer.

The stable yard was empty and so was Colorado's stable. We found Blake in the back field slowly cantering round on the beautiful skewbald with Danny perched in front of him on the pommel of the saddle. They looked so happy and content and in perfect balance. My eyes welled up. This was just too much to take.

As soon as Danny saw his mother he burst into tears and clung on to Blake.

"Come on, Buster, it's time to get down."

"You can come and visit any time, Danny." Sarah was very pale.

"I'll write every week and send you photographs," said Katie miserably.

I gave Danny a hug and realized I couldn't stop trembling. A single magpie scuttered away up the field. One for sorrow . . .

Mrs Mac passed him a bag of food and goodies she'd prepared. "We love you, Danny, and just remember this will always be your home." She stepped aside so that Danny could have one last word with Queenie.

The old pony nuzzled his hair and whickered for a biscuit. When Danny climbed into the car his face was streaked with tears.

"Oh, I nearly forgot." Katie ran forward and pressed her plastic four-leaf clover into his hands. "I want you to have this."

The car rolled out of the drive and out of sight.

"He'll be back," said Sarah, "just wait and see."

The rest of the day dragged by like the last week of term. Katie kept saying that she felt as if half of her was missing, that she was minus an arm or leg. Trevor joked that anybody would think they were an old married couple, but nobody really laughed. Ross made it worse by finding Danny's book, *Black Beauty*, balanced on top of the oven, where he'd obviously forgotten to pick it up.

"We've really got to start applying ourselves." Mrs Mac was breaking out in a rash over the Gala Open Day. "Now here's some notes I've made on the parade, who's going to lead which pony and so on. Ross, I really wish you'd pay attention!"

Sarah was going to read out a brief history of all the rescued horses and ponies over a loudspeaker and we were going to lead them round for everybody to see and admire.

"Timing is going to be essential, and we could really do with more helpers. Any news on the Rocky front?"

All we'd managed to find out was that Rocky had last been seen playing polo on the back of an elephant and had then been rushed to hospital with severe sunburn. Since then, he seemed to have vanished into thin air.

"It's vital we sell as much merchandise as possible." Mrs Mac ticked something else off her list, ignoring the Rocky problem.

The official Hollywell shop, which was once a stable, was now up and running and packed to overflowing. We'd had the inside plastered, a new window put in and a proper door. There was even a cash till.

"I'm expecting big sales of the new baseball caps and Christmas cards. It may only be July but people plan ahead."

Mrs Mac passed round a list of all the craft stalls which were going to be set up in the empty stables – horsehair jewellery, pottery, basket-weaving, sign-writing . . .

"Just so there's no confusion," Ross said, puckering up his brow, "just what is a welly-wanging competition?"

"There's nothing we can do," Sarah insisted later that evening as she broke off from rattling out her next chapter on the electric typewriter. "We can't sit up every night on the edge of a moor waiting for a phantom horse that might never appear. We're needed here at Hollywell Stables."

She had wandered in, looking for her reading glasses which she hated anyone seeing her wearing. She always lost things when she was feeling on edge and since Ross had mentioned the black stallion she'd been positively jumpy. Blake was filling in the entrance form for the local county show and he found the glasses under some papers.

"But this *is* Hollywell business." Ross carried on the argument. "Binny really believes in this stallion."

"So do I, but we can't make it our major priority. What if a real rescue comes in? Bordman Moor is a good hour's drive away. We can't be in two places at once."

"So that's your final word, then?"

"Yes. Of course if Binny sees something else in the meantime, we'll be there like a shot. But we've got to keep a sense of perspective."

I knew Sarah was trying to be sensible. We couldn't stretch ourselves in too many directions, and we still had a sanctuary to run.

"Did you know," Katie read out, "that a horse's

stomach is only the size of a rugby ball, and that's why they can't eat a lot of food at once?"

She was reading from James's veterinary article which had just been printed in the pony magazine *In The Saddle*. James had just dropped it off and we were all incredibly proud. It was the first time his name had appeared in print and he'd kept the whole thing a big secret.

"Or," she went on, "that the kidneys are behind the saddle and the lungs are between the rider's knees?"

"It's a wonder they let us ride them at all." Trevor looked shocked.

"That's because they're noble and majestic creatures," said Sarah.

Rain hammered on the windows like an evil spirit. What had happened to the summer? What had happened to the heatwave?

I stared blankly at a quiz show on television and then switched over to the sheepdog trials. Oscar thought these were a hoot and kept leaping at the screen.

The telephone sat black and ominous in the hallway, as quiet as a Sunday morning.

Sarah plumped up the cushions for the umpteenth time and then decided to drag out the vacuum cleaner which only got used during severe attacks of writer's block.

"We won't hear the phone," Ross bellowed, switching it off at the mains.

"OK, you win, where's her phone number?"

But Katie didn't get a chance to reach for her horsy diary – the phone began to ring, causing us all to leap out of our skins. Sarah picked up the receiver and Binny Alderidge's clipped staccato voice shrilled down the line.

"He's here, he's at the paddock gate – it's the stallion!"

Chapter Four

Binny waved us down at the end of her drive, an oilskin slung over striped pyjamas, rollers clinging precariously to wisps of sodden hair.

"Quick, turn your engine off." She stuck her head through the window. "We don't want to scare him away!"

Sarah immediately switched off the headlights and grabbed her sou'wester. The rain was falling in relentless sheets. At least it managed to muffle any noise we might make.

Slowly, sliding along on the greasy lawn, we edged towards the paddock. The moon was totally hidden by cloud and the only light came from a feeble lamp outside the back porch.

Binny's fingers clutched my arm as a shadow moved in the distance. I only hoped it was a horse and not a burglar. I could feel Blake's warm breath on my neck. We all sounded as if we'd just run a hundred-metre sprint.

"There, I can just make out his ears," said Sarah. "Can you see his head?"

"We need a torch," Blake hissed. "He may run off but we can't do anything in this light."

The deep husky whicker from over by the gate told us all we needed to know.

"Quick, get the torch," Sarah urged.

Ross ran back to the car and Sarah took a couple of steps forward.

"I told you." Excitement caught in Binny's voice. "That's Bordman's Black Beast."

I could practically smell horse sweat and fear in the dank warm air. The hairs on the back of my neck were rising. He was out there, watching us, waiting. Seeing us far better than we could see him.

"He's been there for nearly two hours," Binny whispered. "He wants me to follow him, I know he does."

We heard a squeal and then a hoof stamping. Ross came back with the torch and flickered it towards the gate. "There he is," he murmured. "Look."

The head was well bred, dished, with flared nostrils running into a powerful neck and shoulders. He was as black as charcoal, with a tail so long it was trailing in the mud even though he had it arched over his back like a typical Arab.

"He doesn't look hurt," I said, trying not to move a muscle.

The stallion suddenly trotted off a few paces, stopped, wheeled round and neighed out loud.

"What is it, Blackie, what is it that you want, eh?" Binny shot forward, clinging to the paddock fence, her feet squelching ankle-deep in the mud.

"No!" Trevor, who up to now had been speechless, dived after her. "This is no task for an old lady."

"You're only as old as you feel, now let me go." Binny struggled to free her arms, her voice rising to a screech.

"Don't scare him off." Sarah lunged forward. "For Heaven's sake, this is no time for heroics. Now, Binny, go back into the house. If Angel's out there we'll find her."

"But you don't know the moors." A gust of wind and rain swept the words away like confetti.

"We'll manage. Go inside and ring James. Get the number from the directory – he's on emergency call. Now hurry!"

"Come on," Ross urged. "He won't wait much longer."

We set off across the moors, Ross and Trevor going ahead with Sarah, Blake hanging back, looking after Katie and me.

The stallion kept its distance; it stayed about twenty metres ahead, but trotting back and forth, anxious and fearful, trying to tell us to go faster.

"It's OK, boy, we're going as fast as we can." Sarah tried to settle him. "Just bear with us."

I was shivering like a puppy and sopping wet but it didn't matter. The yellow light of the torch picked up the vast acres of scrubby land pocked with boulders and heather. The wind was icy cold and all around us was barren wasteland; it was so bleak it made my teeth chatter.

"It's not as pretty as it is from the road, is it?" Blake grinned.

"It's wild," I shuddered.

"Anything could happen out here and nobody would know." Katie held on to Blake's hand until her knuckles turned white.

"Whoever dumped that Arab out here needs locking up for ever," Blake's voice was venomous. "Imagine a hot-blooded horse wintering out in this?"

It didn't bear thinking about.

"Where now, Blackie? Come on, you've got to do better than this." Sarah stopped up ahead, her sou'wester tilted to one side and her red hair hanging in drenched rats' tails just like the stallion's.

For half a minute the horse didn't seem to be able to make up his mind. Then he tore down a steep ravine and disappeared from sight.

"Come on, we're going to have to go down."

I slid along on my bottom, grasping clumps of

27

heather as I went. It was sharp and stung my hands but it was better than falling into the unknown.

"Is everyone all right?" Sarah shouted from the bottom, and then let out a shriek of terror.

Ross quickly shone the torch and we vaguely saw the fuzzy figure of a sheep brush up against her leg. We'd stumbled into a whole herd of them.

"They must be sheltering out of the wind," Sarah muttered. "Come on, the stallion's waiting."

We were still going downhill and the ground was getting more and more sodden. My wet socks clamped around my feet like blocks of ice and I didn't think I could go on much further; we must have travelled over two miles.

Suddenly the stallion stopped and started pawing the ground. There was a faint tinkling of water in the shadows and Ross's torch lit up a small stream. And something else . . .

"Oh my God!" Ross's hand started trembling helplessly.

"Don't panic," said Sarah. "Just don't panic."

We clambered forward into the black peat.

"It's OK, little girl, we're on your side." Sarah's voice was honey-smooth and gently coaxing. "We'll soon have you out of there."

A cream-gold head turned to look at her with eyes paralysed by fear. It was Angel.

"How the hell did she get in there?" Trevor couldn't believe it.

Angel was stuck up to her shoulders in thick black cloying peat next to the stream. No matter how frantically she struggled it pulled her down like quicksand and she couldn't move an inch. The rain had soaked her back and neck and her ears were pressed flat against her head. She looked utterly terrified.

"She could have been here for days." Trevor was really shaken.

"She's frozen up." Blake whipped off his jacket and threw it over her back, up to his waist in bog.

"I don't know what to do," said Sarah. "For the first time I haven't got a clue how I'm supposed to handle this."

"I don't want to speak out of turn, Mrs F, but I think we might need the fire brigade."

"Yeah, Trevor's right." Blake fought his way back to us, his shirt already rain-soaked. "I've seen something like this happen once before, and they had to lift the horse out in a sling."

"We need James." Sarah was desperately trying to get a grip. "Someone's going to have to find their way back to Binny's."

I ran full pelt across the moors towards the flickering light in the distance. Ross was just behind me, gasping for breath, stumbling, cursing, trying to go faster – Angel's life was in our hands.

Seeing the Land Rover bumping over the rough ground towards us was like seeing the star over Bethlehem.

"Ross, look, it's James!" My face became streaked with rain as I stood heaving for breath.

"What's happened, where is everyone?" James's soft brown eyes were filled with panic.

"It's all right," Ross wheezed, holding his hands on his knees. "Nobody's hurt." And he then told James the whole story.

"Ross, go back to Binny's. Get the fire brigade, we'll need at least two crews. Tell Binny to get some warm blankets. Hurry! Mel, you're coming with me!"

I clambered into the back of the Land Rover behind the driver, a mountain of a man with a thick beard.

James quickly introduced him: "This is Binny's neighbour, Jimmy. Now which way?"

James sank into the deep bog up to his armpits. Blake followed, holding up the black medical bag.

"Be careful," Sarah shouted, her eyes never leaving James's back. I felt exactly the same about Blake.

Jimmy angled the Land Rover so that the headlights shone on Angel. She was transfixed with fear, like a startled rabbit. In the distance, the stallion whickered and snorted, pacing up and down then stopping and tossing his head. There was no way he was going to leave Angel.

"It's all right, little love, just stay calm." James gently ran his hand down Angel's sweating neck.

We stood watching, huddling together for warmth, Sarah, Trevor, Katie, me and Jimmy – without Jimmy I don't think we'd have ever got the Land Rover down into the ravine. He knew a back route and handled the terrain like a pro.

"Why don't you sit in the Land Rover?" he said to Katie and Sarah. "We're going to be here a long time yet."

James was feeling all over Angel's body, running his hands over her back, loins and flanks. The bog had her legs and most of her underside totally submerged in an evil grip, but at least she hadn't sunk down any further. James inched round to her tail and Blake passed him the thermometer. The lights from the Land Rover were a godsend as James gave Angel an internal examination.

"What is it, what's wrong?" Sarah's voice rose sharply.

"Listen." Katie held her breath. "They're here!"

The blue lights suddenly came into view, following the path Jimmy had taken. Five firefighters leapt out of the first engine and ploughed across to us. Two other engines pulled in behind it.

"Angel!" Binny appeared from nowhere, clutching a pile of blankets. She was horrified when she saw her, and I could actually see the old lady start to shake.

"It's not as bad as it looks." Sarah put an arm round her but didn't sound very convincing.

"Angel, sweetheart!" Binny's voice rose and cracked.

Blake waved at her and Angel looked up and squealed delightedly.

"Come on, I think you ought to get into the Land Rover, you'll catch your death out here." Jimmy manhandled her into the front seat next to Katie. "Now don't argue with me, Binny, I know what's best."

James pushed his way back through the bog, leaving Blake by Angel's head, keeping her calm. Two firefighters grabbed hold of his bag and an arm each and dragged him free. He was plastered in mud right up to his shoulders and was even spitting it out of his mouth.

"How is she? Tell me the truth, I want it laid on the line." Binny strained her head out of the Land Rover window, suddenly looking very old.

"She's extremely weak, Binny. I think she's been

there for a couple of days." James's voice was soft, gentle, a medical voice, and a cold finger of dread ran up my spine.

"I'm going to put her on a drip and give her some cortisone and Finadyne, to help reduce the shock and any pain—" James broke off and glanced towards the stallion who was still hovering by the edge of the trees.

"But?" Binny urged.

"There's an added complication."

"Well, tell me, then. Don't drag it out."

"She's in foal. It's on its way!"

Chapter Five

"She's in the very first stages of labour, so it's going to be a while yet."

Jimmy was gripping hold of Binny's hand.

"But it doesn't look good, I'm afraid. It's a breech. The foal's coming out backwards."

Binny's face contorted with shock, her eyes disbelieving. "She's twenty years old and it's her first foal."

"I know," James answered. "But she still has a chance."

And it was that chance, that single ray of hope which kept us all going.

Ross eventually swapped places with Blake at Angel's head where he'd been trying to keep her calm. Blake trudged over to the Land Rover, mud-blackened and exhausted. "I don't know how Angel's standing it," he whispered to me out of earshot of Binny. "It's a nightmare out there."

I'd got my fingers crossed for good luck and Sarah sent Jimmy and Binny back to the house to make flasks of tea, in the hope that it would take her mind off Angel. The firefighters were using Jimmy's chainsaw to cut down some trees so they could manœuvre the engines nearer to the bog.

"Time's running out," Blake whispered. "We've got to get her out of there."

I wiped a smear of mud from the corner of his mouth, then he went back to help Ross.

It was vital to get the drip into Angel as soon as possible, and James gathered his equipment together. "I only hope this works," he said.

"It will." Sarah was being a hundred and ten per cent positive.

Trevor came back from the tree-cutting with specks of wet sawdust all over his face.

Angel had sunk deeper into the bog. It was now up to her neck.

"Let her be all right." Katie clung on to my hand.

The options weren't very hopeful. They could either pull her straight out, which would endanger her life, or they could try and get hold of a crane and hoist her out. Either way it wasn't going to be easy.

Jimmy and Binny came back from the house with flasks of tea, which were over-sugared, but it didn't really seem to matter.

"It's no good pretending," she snapped. "I might

be old but I'm not stupid. I know it doesn't look good."

At least the drip was working. Angel had started to perk up and even tried to neigh to the stallion, who was still hanging around, unsure as to what was going on.

"See, where there's life there's hope." Jimmy put an arm round Binny's shoulder.

"I don't need your philosophy on life, Jimmy. If you want to be useful, just say a prayer."

"We'll get her out, you know, love," said one of the firefighters. "We haven't lost one yet."

But they didn't know anything about horses, and Angel must be getting exhausted.

It continued to pour with rain and we could barely see what was going on. Nobody seemed quite sure what to do, and there was still no way of getting the fire engines nearer to the bog. One of the firefighters tried to locate a crane on his mobile phone but everyone eventually agreed that the ground was just too wet. They'd never get it anywhere near the bog.

"So what do we do?" Binny was panicking. "We can't just sit here like lemons and watch her suffer."

"It's no good losing your temper, Binny. These gentlemen are doing their best." Jimmy tried to put a coat round her shoulders, but she shook it off.

"She's my little baby." Binny put a hand up to her face, the tears streaming down her cheeks. "I can't stand it any longer, I should be with her." She pushed past two of the firefighters and stumbled forward.

"Binny, don't be so stupid. Leave it to the professionals." Jimmy whipped her round like a rag doll and dragged her back towards the Land Rover. "All we can do is wait," he said. "That vet knows what he's doing and so do these guys. Now trust me, she's going to be all right." Jimmy wrapped his huge arms round her frail body and wouldn't let go until she'd stopped crying. "Now, come on, you silly old goose, let's just try and think positive – for Angel's sake."

"Jimmy O'Connor, don't you dare call me a silly old goose."

"Now that's more like it," Jimmy chuckled. "Mel, what about a cup of tea for this OAP?"

Another hour dragged by. Blake brought the empty drip bag and coil back up to the Land Rover but it didn't look good. When I asked him how she was, he just shook his head.

"See, I told you," Binny murmured.

Sarah was being a real brick, laughing and joking with the firefighters and trying to keep up morale. They'd managed to get an engine within a few metres of the bog, with the idea of putting a rope round Angel's neck and dragging her out. But James eventually decided it was too dangerous.

"The vet's coming out," said Jimmy, and I could just make out James being pulled out of the bog by two firefighters. "Now we'll find out what's going on."

Sarah gave James a cup of tea and he drank it all in one go. His hands were blue with the cold.

"She's improved enormously in the last half hour. The drip's done its work and she's certainly stronger. But we've got to move fast. Time's running out, and we've got to get her out of there."

The firefighters pressed round to listen to James's plan.

"There's going to be a lot of kicking and thrashing," he continued. "The main thing is that no one gets hurt, so we've all got to work together. She's a lot calmer now. I think it's possible."

All the firefighters were going to move into the bog and try to lift Angel out. It was bizarre but James said it was the only way. He was worried that the foal was lodged in such a position that it might suffocate. He had to do something.

"If we can just give her a kick-start," James said, "if we could just get the front legs out, she might be able to do the rest herself."

"I'm going in with you." Jimmy stripped off his jacket and marched forward.

"Jimmy, don't be a fool, what about your rheumatism?"

He wouldn't listen. "I'm going in whether you like it or not. I wasn't called mammoth muscles for nothing, you know."

"No, but that was twenty years ago," said Binny, arching her eyebrows at him.

"OK guys, are we ready?"

Six firefighters got behind Angel and four on either side. She might only be thirteen hands but she would still be incredibly heavy. Added to which there would be suction from the bog. Even with all that manpower it was an incredible task.

Binny was wringing her hands together in desperation. "What do you think, Mel, has she got a chance?"

They all heaved together. It was a massive effort. I could just make out Angel's head and her ears flicking back and forth. She looked as if she was fighting for her life.

"Come on, Angel, you can do it!" Binny clutched my arm.

"Come on, Angel," screamed Katie, at the top of her voice.

For seconds all we could hear was scrabbling, paddling noises, grunting and heaving. Trevor and Jimmy were right in the thick of it.

"I can't see anything," said Binny, frantic with frustration.

Someone yelled out. Then we heard a thud.

"Someone's hurt," I yelled.

It was pandemonium. Angel was plunging all over the place. Men were falling back into the bog.

"What's happening?" Binny shrieked.

"She's out!" Sarah went berserk. "Look, you can see her shoulders."

Angel made a last valiant effort and dragged herself on to firm ground.

A huge whoop went up from the firefighters and Trevor punched the air with his fist.

"She's out!" Binny screeched and hugged Sarah violently. We were all leaping around, tears mingling with the rain, emotion brimming over. "I don't believe it," Binny cried. "I thought I was going to lose her."

James and Blake were at Angel's head, examining her as we ran towards them.

"I should have brought a Jammy Dodger," said Binny. "She loves Jammy Dodgers."

"There'll be plenty of time for that later," said Sarah. "Let's see how she is first."

Angel was standing with her head down, trembling all over, her cream coat blackened and her tail a wet wisp. She looked so bony and pathetic

40

it made my eyes sting. James was feeling over her stomach and looking in her eyes.

As we went towards her Binny was overcome. "Oh my poor little baby, what's happened to you?" She reached out her hand and touched the soft pink nose. "Remember me, girl, it's been a long time, hasn't it?"

Angel turned her head, stared at Binny and then dropped her nose and sniffed at her sweater. A flood of recognition lit up her eyes and she started whickering excitedly, lifting up one of her forelegs, and then the other.

"She's always done that," Binny said. "Frank taught her years ago and she's never forgotten it."

"Horses never forget anything," Sarah grinned. "Especially people – they always remember a good deed, and a bad one for that matter."

Binny kissed the pink nose and brushed away fresh tears. "I always knew you were alive," she whispered. "I never gave up on you, Angel, not for one second."

James gave me a worried glance and reached for the stethoscope. All the firefighters crowded round, quiet and anxious, wondering what was going to happen next.

"I've got to deliver the foal here," James announced. "There's no time."

It wasn't long before Angel lay down on her

side. Binny took off her coat and pressed it under her head but she was in too much pain to notice.

It was then that we heard the stallion screaming out from under some distant trees. He reared up and pawed the air as if to say he was worried about Angel too. Up until that point we had completely forgotten about him – we'd been too busy trying to save Angel's life.

"He is the father, after all," Ross said. "He's got a right to be concerned."

"While he's still hanging around," James said, "it might be an idea to contact the local zoo for a marksman. We can't leave him here."

"James is right," Sarah said. "Somehow we've got to get them both back to Hollywell and a newborn foal as well."

"Which is just starting to make its way into the world," James said, examining Angel.

At least the rain had stopped, and the firefighters drove the three engines towards us so they acted as a windbreak and gave James more light.

"Now then, my little girl," James stroked Angel's damp coat, "let's see if we can do this together, shall we?"

Usually a foal is positioned with its forelegs forward, and these come out first with the head following and then the rest of the body. Angel's foal was completely twisted the wrong way. Somehow

James had to push the foal back in, grab the hoof of a hindleg and flex and pull it into the right position. He explained this as he was working but I still couldn't picture in my mind what he was trying to do.

"It's OK, darling, I'm here." Binny crouched down next to Angel's head. "Mummy's here, it's going to be all right."

I'd never watched a birth before apart from on television and it was hard to imagine a new life was about to appear.

"I hope it's a girl," Katie said, watching eagerly.

"Katie, I don't know whether you should be watching this." Sarah was concerned.

"It's educational," Katie said. "Besides, Trevor's the squeamish one."

"I am not."

"Well, I don't care if it's a boy or a girl," said Binny. "I just want Angel to be all right."

"We all do, Binny." Sarah put a hand on her arm. "We all do."

Angel half lifted her head and then gave a huge sigh. She was sweating more now, and Binny was wiping her eyes and nose with the corner of her sweater. "Hang in there, darling, it'll soon be over."

James was working like mad to try and correct the breech, but it was still no good. "Come on,

Angel, don't fight against me." Everybody was willing her on.

Minutes ticked past and there was still no progress. James once told us that unlike humans, foals are often born very fast, in as little as ten to fifteen minutes. It was only because Angel had problems that it was taking this long.

"It's no good." James looked up and across to Binny. Rain, mud and sweat ran down his face. "It's the worst breech I've ever seen. I hate to tell you this, Binny, but I think we're going to lose the foal."

A huge wave of hopelessness swept over me. Angel couldn't have come through all this for her foal to die, fate couldn't be that cruel. Katie gripped my hand and I knew she was thinking the same thing.

"Keep trying, James." Sarah's eyes were desperate.

"Just save Angel." Binny stroked the drenched cream-coloured coat. "Do what you have to do but don't let her die."

A short distance away the stallion paced up and down, neighing every so often. He looked defeated, as if it was all his fault.

James went back to work.

We all waited.

Binny was stroking Angel over and over. I

wondered how she'd cope if she lost both the foal and Angel. Oh please, God, save them. It just wasn't fair. It would be too much of a tragedy for anyone to bear.

Suddenly a huge grin burst across James's face. He was scrabbling for extra leverage, his whole body stretched out on the ground. "I've got it!" he yelled. "I've got the leg, the foal's still alive!"

"Yippee!" Katie shouted and everybody started cheering and clapping and then just as quickly fell quiet again. There was still work to do.

"Look!" Katie's mouth opened in astonishment. A tiny nose and head had just appeared. It was so beautiful. It was the foal. It was being born!

The next few minutes were magical. I wasn't a bit squeamish. I just couldn't take my eyes off that tiny bundle of life.

"You've done it, girl," Binny shrieked. "You've done it!" Angel lifted her head and then sank down again.

But something was wrong. The foal wasn't moving.

James went to work like a shot. "It's not breathing."

With cool calm efficiency, he yanked the body up by its hind legs, shaking it, slapping it, then rubbing its tiny body. "Come on." Vital seconds ticked by. "Come on!" James started blowing into its nostrils, giving it the kiss of life.

"Breathe, please breathe," I prayed.

Suddenly it gave a couple of spasmodic gasps and a shudder, then it struggled on to its side. Each breath was shallow and weak at first but then it grew stronger.

James sank back on his knees, looking close to collapse. "It's a filly!" he grinned. "A chestnut filly."

A huge whoop went up from all the firefighters and everybody started shaking hands and slapping each other's backs.

"Where's Trevor?" Katie said, and then we saw him stretched out unconscious like a felled tree. "I think he's fainted!"

The next few moments were truly beautiful. Gingerly the newborn foal tried to find its legs, all spindly and giraffe-like, and James eased it round to its mother's milk.

"The mother's first milk is vital," Katie informed the firefighters. "It's called the colostrum and stops the foal getting germs." She never could resist the chance to show off.

"She's so tiny." Binny couldn't take her eyes off the foal.

James rubbed her dry with a towel and Angel

started taking an interest, watching, whickering, eyes filling up with motherly love.

"Sssssh." James held a finger to his lips as the foal wobbled towards Angel's head. Nearly, nearly, and then plopped to the ground. Angel looked almost shy and then reached out her nose and sniffed the tiny damp ears.

Reassured, the foal thrust her face into Angel's as if to say, "Hi, Mum, it's me, I've arrived."

"Isn't it wonderful?" I was almost choked up as I whispered to Blake.

Binny tenderly reached out and touched the delicate tapered nose and dinky little ears.

"She's a little beauty." Blake bent down next to Binny and put an arm round her shoulders.

He told her that it was in the first hour of life that you could tell a future champion. After that it was difficult to predict because they were constantly changing shape. "This little mite is up with the best of them," Blake said. "There will be nothing to outclass her, you can take my word on that."

I felt my body tingle all over. It was a special moment for all of us.

"Two for the price of one," Binny laughed. "But how am I going to cope?"

We decided to give mother and daughter a few moments to themselves and collapsed inside the

Land Rover completely exhausted. James wiped his hands clean and Binny kept saying how could she ever thank him. Sarah told her to be careful or it would all go to his head.

"What I wouldn't give for a hot bath now," Sarah groaned, trying to wring her hair dry with a paper tissue then giving up. All the towels Binny had brought from the house were soaked and the only thing I could find in the Land Rover was a ragged bit of oily sack which Ross said wasn't much use to man nor beast.

"I propose a toast," Sarah said through chattering teeth, holding up a mug of stone-cold tea. She pushed open the Land Rover door and yelled out, "To the best firefighting team in the country – well done, lads."

"Hear, hear." Katie backed her up and there was a general chorus of grunts and groans and an anguished yelp from Jimmy who'd hurt his leg in the bog and not said a word until now when he'd turned green with pain.

"Probably a chipped bone," James announced. And Jimmy shrugged it off, saying it was all in the line of duty.

"This will probably go down as one of the most incredible rescue operations of all time." Ross put the plastic lid back on one of the flasks.

"We're bound to be on television." Katie's eyes glinted.

"Oh, not again." Ross put a hand to his forehead in mock despair. "But seriously," he went on, "the discovery of the real Black Beast after all this time is bound to cause a sensation."

James gave both Angel and the foal a shot of antibiotics, and the firefighters took one last look then climbed into their vehicles. But not before Sarah had given them our address and made them all promise devoutly to come to our Gala Open Day.

"What about transport?" Sarah said when the last engine disappeared from sight. The thought of moving an exhausted mare, a newborn foal and a wild horse back to Hollywell was daunting. It would take far too long to fetch our horsebox. Jimmy came to the rescue with the suggestion that he hitch his trailer to the Land Rover for Angel and the foal and then he had a cattle wagon we could use for the stallion. It sounded like a good plan.

"Always handy to know a farmer," Binny winked.

Sarah said she'd drive the lorry if Binny could manage the Land Rover. Jimmy would have to go with them because he couldn't remember where he'd put the lorry keys.

49

"Hang on a minute." James punched out the number for Bordman Zoo on his mobile phone to find out exactly what was going on. Every minute that ticked by I imagined the stallion would disappear.

Relief spread over James's face. "You'll have to stop off at Binny's cottage. Look out for a white van. It's the marksman," he said. "He's on his way!"

Chapter Six

It wasn't going to be easy.

The stallion stood hunched under the trees, oily-black from the constant rain, his hindquarters bunched up and his legs splayed out in the mud. Ross and Blake had tried to get near him earlier but he'd backed off immediately, his ears pressed flat and his tail swishing. He hardly ever took his eyes off Angel and the foal.

"The poor thing," I said. "He's got nobody, he's so alone."

Almost as if he heard me, the stallion pawed at the ground and neighed to Angel, but she was busy nuzzling the foal who was still trying to stand up.

"He's not very friendly." I think Katie had been imagining a Black Beauty lookalike who, after leading us to Angel, would happily let us catch him and live happily ever after at Hollywell Stables.

James was convinced that he'd hardly had any contact with humans, that he'd probably been left in a field since he was a foal. It was the only explanation. I must admit, I didn't think there were many horses who would pass up the chance of some food and shelter in preference to a cold desolate moor. Even the wild Dartmoor and New Forest ponies were tamer than this.

"I'll tell you something for nothing," said the marksman, who had arrived ten minutes earlier and was busy loading the special rifle. "You've got your work cut out there. I've never seen a horse with such a look about him – he wouldn't trust his own shadow."

"If it wasn't for him my Angel wouldn't be in this state." Binny was getting more and more anxious. Angel still hadn't got to her feet and the foal was clamouring for more milk.

Trevor was helping the marksman set up a special battery-operated floodlight. It was all being done in a matter of minutes but it seemed to take for ever.

We were trying to be as quiet as possible but I knew the stallion was getting suspicious. He kept looking from us to Angel and pacing up and down, tossing his head and snorting with distrust.

"He's a strong fella. I'd say it's going to take ten to fifteen minutes for him to go down." The marksman explained how the dart had to hit the top of a hind leg where there was the largest muscle mass. He was going to use an anaesthetic called Immobilon which would knock him out completely. "We won't switch the light on until the very last minute."

The tension was unbearable.

"As soon as he drops, we'll get a rope round his neck." James folded the rope like a lasso.

I'd never seen a horse being darted before. I didn't know what would happen.

James said if we didn't catch him now, we might never have another chance. It was nearly imposs- ible to catch a wild horse on an open moor and the only reason he was hanging around at the moment was because of Angel. It was now or never.

"So does everybody know what they've got to do?" As soon as the stallion was hit we were to spread out in a circle and try to keep him from charging off until the anaesthetic started to work. "It won't take long," the marksman said.

"Everybody ready?" James fiddled with the switch on the floodlight and suddenly a whole clump of trees was illuminated, dazzling the stal- lion who wheeled round, squealing in fright, won- dering what on earth was happening.

"It's OK, boy," I whispered under my breath. "We've got to be cruel to be kind."

The marksman closed his fingers on the trigger and the first dart went sailing out. "Blast, it's no good, the lamp's frightening him. We'll have to

53

wait for daylight." The marksman clambered to his feet in defeat.

"No." James was adamant. "We can't wait that long. I want Angel in a dry stable as soon as possible. We haven't got another two hours. Please, at least give it another try."

The marksman shrugged his shoulders and loaded another dart.

"We've got to catch him," James urged. "There's no two ways about it. He's got to go back to Hollywell."

Sarah squeezed my hand and our hearts thumped anxiously. Some distance away, Jimmy sat in the rusty cattle wagon waiting. That would be another nightmare – how to get the stallion up the ramp?

"Ssssh," Blake hissed, looking to where the stallion was tentatively moving out from under the trees. One step at a time, getting closer to Angel.

"Here's our chance," James whispered. "Let's not blow it."

The marksman knelt down and took aim. It was a clean, perfectly targeted shot and the stallion cried out with anger and fear.

"Blimey, he's going crazy," Trevor shouted.

I'd never seen a horse react like it: he was carrying on like a bronco.

"We've got him! Come on, move in on him quick!" said James, as he and Blake ran forward.

Somehow Binny managed to trip over the cable to the floodlight and it blacked out, leaving us all in complete darkness. I heard the stallion fall and scrabble to his feet again.

My feet squelched and pulled in the mud and I could hardly see where I was going.

"Where's Mel?" It was Blake's voice, anxiety filtering through. "She's not here!"

Trevor bawled in the distance. "He's all over the place! It's not working!"

The stallion appeared from nowhere, a black solid shape coming out of the darkness with his head down and his teeth bared. He was staggering about, foaming at the mouth, gasping for breath, but it didn't stop him. He just kept heading straight at me, charging like a bull.

"Mel!"

It suddenly dawned on me that I'd wandered between the stallion and Angel. I remembered from wildlife programmes that that was something you should never do.

"Mel, run!" I heard Blake's voice but my legs just froze like two concrete posts. It was all happening in slow motion. I couldn't do a thing about it. The dart should be working, why wasn't the dart working?

"Melanie!"

Stone-cold fear clogged my throat. I couldn't scream, I couldn't breathe, I couldn't move. He was going to kill me.

Blake's body hit mine just seconds before the stallion would have run me over. We both went hurtling to the ground in a rugby tackle and my head fell back against a jagged stone with a sickening thud.

"Melanie!" I could feel Blake's breath on my neck and his eyes boring down on me. "Melanie, don't do this to me!"

Blood started slowly seeping down my neck and I tried to smile but then a black wave engulfed me and all I could do was lie there and listen to a voice from far away.

"She's unconscious!"

I woke up in my own room at Hollywell, staring at a picture of Milton, the famous show-jumper, and wondering what on earth had happened. My head felt on fire and I couldn't stop shivering, and then the realization hit me like a ton of bricks. The stallion; the hospital; waiting around for what seemed hours for X-ray results; Sarah worried and strained; Blake carrying me into Casualty with a strip of his shirt pressed against my head. It was all coming back – every gory detail.

I plumped up the pillows and winced as a stab of pain shot up my neck. Someone had opened the window and there was a massive display of carnations on my bedside table. Propped up against the vase was a sherbet-lemon-coloured card which read in bold type: "Get Better Soon. From all your fans at Hollywell." There was a cat's paw mark in one corner which looked suspiciously like Oscar's.

"So you're awake, then. It's about time." Blake poked his head round the door, giving me a huge smile. "We all thought you were auditioning for Sleeping Beauty."

He sauntered into the room, grinning boyishly, and I suddenly became aware of my sticking-up hair and washed-out pyjamas, and sank further under the duvet feeling very self-conscious. He then told me how Binny had made up some kind of herbal concoction and I'd been sleeping it off ever since.

"It completely zonked you out," he said. "We could hear you snoring for hours."

I nearly hit the roof when he told me I'd slept solidly through the next day and night and it was now the following morning.

"But how could you let me stay in bed this long?

And where's Angel, and what's happened to the stallion?" I tried to move my legs but they felt like planks of wood.

"Whoa, whoa, one thing at a time." Blake stood over me, suddenly really worried and I knew I looked terrible. I forced a smile but my face felt like cardboard.

"Angel and the foal are in the intensive care unit and Blackie's round the back kicking Queenie's stable to smithereens. There's nothing to worry about."

"So why does my throat feel like sandpaper and why can't I stop shivering?" I didn't tell Blake that I felt sick too.

"The doc says you've got a temperature after all that rain. Trevor's just as bad – he's walking round like a bear with a sore head."

"So nothing's changed, then." My head felt as if a hundred little hammers were drilling away inside it.

"I'll go and fetch Sarah," Blake said, concern still etched on his face. "Remember, you've had a nasty knock. You've got to take it easy."

"Yes, sir." I saluted him, and then felt dizzy and wished I hadn't moved so suddenly. My mouth felt as if I'd got fungus growing on my teeth, and my head was about to blow off my shoulders.

"Oh, and by the way," Blake said as he levered

himself out of the chair, "you look just like normal."

I threw the pillow at him and he dived out of the door just as it clipped off my prize cactus.

A few minutes later Sarah led a small procession in to check on me.

"Mel, you've got to take this seriously," Sarah said. "You can't just get knocked out and then act as if nothing's happened."

I was trying to get out of bed but somehow my legs wouldn't co-operate.

Trevor followed Katie in, his nose throbbing like a bright red hooter and a huge length of toilet roll screwed up in one hand. "I can't breathe," he groaned. "I feel terrible."

Sarah told him to be a man and put a thermometer into my mouth.

"I'm getting up whether you like it or not," I squeaked.

There was a cool breeze outside and it brought me round no end as we approached Angel's stable.

"Ssssh, don't make too much noise." Trevor tiptoed closer to the stable door looking like a proud father.

The foal was sucking hungrily at Angel's milk

and swishing her short fluffy tail. She looked as if she'd grown a foot since last time I'd seen her.

"She's going to be a right little madam," Sarah said, reaching for the water bucket to refill it. Angel looked exhausted but never once lost her temper with the foal, who wouldn't leave her alone for a second.

"James said she might turn grey in a few months," Katie whispered excitedly. "He said it's more than likely with a Palomino mother. I didn't know they could change colour."

The foal stared at Katie with huge brown eyes and then scuttled round the back of Angel and peered out from underneath her tummy. She looked so comical that we all burst out laughing.

"I don't think she knew that either," Ross said. "You'll be giving her a complex."

I insisted on seeing the stallion.

"I'm not sure you should." Blake and Ross exchanged worried glances but it was too late, I was already shuffling round to Queenie's stable.

What I saw filled me with cold dread. I'd never seen a horse look so angry, so mean and distrusting. His eyes were like empty shells and as soon as I put my head over the door he ran at me with his yellow teeth snapping.

"I did try to warn you." Blake rearranged the metal grille which covered the top half of the door to stop him jumping out.

"He's sedated at the moment." Ross came up behind me. "He was literally climbing up the walls when we first put him in here. James was nearly crushed to death."

The stallion started kicking out at the breeze-block walls, as if to reinforce what Ross had just said. His coat was dull and brittle and most likely infested with lice. There were spiky burrs stuck in his mane and tail, and his nose was scratched and bleeding.

"So what aren't you telling me?" I knew Ross and Blake probably better than anyone else in the world and it was as plain as day that they were hiding something.

Ross shuffled his feet and Blake stared out over the paddocks.

"Has he got some disease or something?" Sweat was running in rivulets down my back and my hands suddenly felt clammy.

"James told us . . ." Ross broke off, looking awkward.

"James said what?"

"Mel, you've got to be rational about this. It's no good getting all sentimental."

"Ross, will you stop talking in riddles and tell me what's going on?"

"He might have to be put down." Blake almost spat out the words. "He's dangerous and quite frankly I agree with James, he's got no place at Hollywell Stables."

"I don't believe you've just said that." Blood rushed to my head and I staggered to keep my balance. "How could you even think such a thing?"

"For God's sake, Mel." Blake spun round. "He nearly killed you!"

"But he didn't, did he? I'm still here. He deserves a chance. That's what we're here for, to help horses that nobody else wants, not to give in as soon as we come up against a hurdle."

"He's not a hurdle, Mel, he's crazy." Ross was right on Blake's side.

"I don't care what you both think, it's not going to happen, not if I can help it." I turned on my heel, fury pumping at my temples, and suddenly felt my knees give way like jelly beneath me.

"Will you stop being so flaming stubborn." Blake scooped me up in his arms just as I was about to crumple in a heap, and started carrying me towards the house. "You shouldn't even be out of bed. Now shut up for at least two minutes and do as you're told."

Ross ran on ahead and opened the back door

and Sarah came rushing through from the hallway looking worried sick.

"I'm OK, it's just Blake making a fuss," I gasped, and was then overcome by another wave of nausea.

"Trevor, phone the doctor. I knew something like this would happen. Blake, take her upstairs. I'll get a hot-water bottle."

The doctor arrived and immediately prescribed antibiotics and bed rest. Trevor was seriously miffed that he'd just got a common cold.

Jigsaw lay on the end of the bed licking my feet and whining endlessly as if it was all too sad for words. Katie brought me some pony magazines and half a chocolate egg. I sat there fuming, not interested in anything but the stallion and what was going to happen to him. Sarah refused to talk about it.

Blake brought me some watery scrambled eggs and stood staring at me as if he had something deep and meaningful to say. We had another row about the stallion and then he said he'd come back when I'd calmed down, which would probably be the end of the next century.

Trevor slunk into my room, hovering by the bed

looking more bunged up than ever. I was getting so many visitors it felt like Piccadilly Circus.

"So he's told you, then?" Trevor shuffled nervously. "No, not about the stallion," he added. "About the job offer." My face must have frozen over. "Why does something tell me I've put my foot in it?" Trevor was turning purple.

"Not one foot, Trevor, both of them."

Blake stood with his back to me, looking out of the window, struggling to find the right words.

"I was going to tell you, Mel, but I didn't know how to and there never seemed to be the right moment."

He'd been offered a job in Ireland, in one of the top show-jumping yards, where he'd get to ride some of the best horses in the world.

"It's a fantastic opportunity, it could make all the difference to my career. I'd be a fool to pass it up."

Scalding hot tears burnt at the back of my eyes and my head throbbed.

"I'd be leaving in a week's time," he added.

I felt as if somebody had just punched me in the stomach.

"It sounds as if you've already made up your mind."

He gave me one of his probing looks but I kept my eyes down and refused to look at him.

"How long have you known?"

"Three weeks."

"And you've only just decided to tell me?" I was incredulous. It was the fact that I had to hear it from Trevor that really hurt.

"It wasn't like that," he said. "I didn't want to hurt you."

"Well, you have all right, so I hope you're satisfied."

"I don't know what to say."

"Don't say anything," I spluttered. "Just go, please, just leave me alone."

I didn't think he was going to take any notice. Long seconds dragged past and he made no effort to move. I could feel his eyes burning into my face looking for any sign that I might not mean it. But I did. I couldn't stand being in the same room as him. I felt utterly betrayed.

"Well, if that's what you want . . ."

"Yes."

"OK, then." He marched out, the door clicking shut behind him. I heard his footsteps on the stairs. He was gone.

I turned and buried my head under the pillow just like I used to when I was small and had no control over anything that was happening.

I didn't hear Katie sneak into the room, not until she'd come across and perched on the end of the bed, fiddling with my stuffed toys and looking as desolate as I felt.

"Sarah's just been speaking to Mrs Barrat," she said. "Apparently Danny's having a wonderful time and didn't want to come to the phone. He won't be visiting in the holidays."

I squeezed her hand and forced back a sob which was stifling my throat.

"You know," Katie said, "Trevor's right. Sometimes life can be really unfair."

Chapter Seven

The next couple of days were fraught with emotion. I was barely talking to Blake, and Katie was wandering around like a lost sheep.

Sarah had agreed to give the stallion another week to see if there was any improvement, providing only James or Blake went near him. At the moment he wasn't eating anything and would soon be as weak as a kitten. Even so, James said he'd never seen a horse so vicious. Blake had to literally chuck some hay into the stable while Ross held the stallion back with the yard brush. The only way we could get to the water bucket was by feeding in the hosepipe. It only went to prove that at some stage in his life the stallion must have been grossly mistreated.

On top of all this, the old-fashioned tractor we used for moving the manure collapsed completely and even Trevor couldn't do anything with it. Everybody had to spend hours extra pushing wheelbarrow after wheelbarrow, and all the loose straw blowing around made the place look more like a farm.

Walter and Arnie escaped twice to the local pub, the Whistle and Pig, where the landlord gave them Guinness by the bucketful. They were becoming a familiar sight wandering around the pavements, a wily mule and a seventeen-hand Hanoverian dressage horse. Sarah said we'd have to put them in strait-jackets before the week was out.

The whole structure of our lives seemed to be breaking down into chaotic bedlam. And all the time I was ticking off the days until Blake's departure. How could he turn his back on us like this?

The Gala Open Day was now only a week away. The paddock cum car-park was a mud bath and three of the craft stalls had pulled out at the last minute. The burger bar had also pulled out, going instead to a big three-day event in the next county. We were stuck with no refreshments apart from cream teas, and hundreds of people to entertain. It couldn't get much worse.

And then Angel started having problems. James said she wasn't providing enough milk for the foal. He was going to try a course of treatment but in the meantime there was only one option. We'd have to handfeed the foal.

He brought us a supply of dried mare's milk substitute and two bottles with teats. It was going to be a major job.

"She needs a feed every two hours, day and night." James was grim-faced. "It's going to be a heck of a task."

It was touch and go as to whether the hormonal injections James had given her would bring down her milk. James said if it didn't he would contact the "foaling bank", which was a system designed to locate a foster mum somewhere in the country, a mare who had recently lost her own foal and might adopt Angel's. We all hoped it wouldn't come to that but as each day went past it seemed more likely.

I was now beginning to understand why Angel looked so tired. After the first two nights of hand-feeding we were all walking round with huge dark bags under our eyes. The foal was loving every minute of it and I'd managed to talk Sarah into letting me do my bit. I was feeling a lot better although still really shaky and I'd lost half a stone in weight.

It was three o'clock on the third night when I crept downstairs to join Trevor in Angel's stable. We'd put her in the intensive care unit because it was twice the size of a normal stable and had special heated lights. It was also nearest to the house and Trevor had rigged up a sound system so we could hear the slightest noise. Mrs Mac had been terrified when Trevor first switched it on and she heard Angel munching at some hay – it sounded as if it was coming from directly behind the sofa.

The kitchen floor felt like the North Pole under my bare feet and I quickly pulled on my wellies and glided across the yard as quietly as I could. Boris, our old hunter, was snoring so loudly it was amazing he didn't bring down the rafters.

"Trevor, is that you?" I poked my head over the door, shivering from head to foot but glad to be doing my shift with Trevor and not Blake.

Angel was lying at the back of the stable resting, her heavy eyelids flicking open every now and then to watch us. She really was the most lovely pony with a sweet nature. When she arrived we'd spent hours brushing off the thick black peatish mud and had to literally pick it off her stomach but she hadn't minded one bit and had looked so incredibly grateful.

The foal swished her tail and started trying to eat Trevor's hair. I pulled an apple quarter out of my pocket and offered it to Angel.

"You know, Mel, you can talk to me, we're supposed to be friends." Trevor always had a way of getting right to the heart of what I was thinking. I couldn't hide anything from him.

"I just can't believe he'd go off to Ireland like

70

that," I blurted out. "After all we've done for him, after all we've been through."

Trevor quietly watched me, letting it all come out, letting me pour out all my thoughts and feelings. Just being a good listener, a best friend.

"I don't know what to say to him any more, Trevor, it's like there's a brick wall between us." I bent down and stroked the foal who was staring at me with huge brown eyes, sensing that something was wrong.

"He's a show-jumper, Mel. He wants to get to the top. He's got something to prove, to himself and to the world. If Ireland can give him the chance to do that, then he's got to take it. If he doesn't he might regret it for the rest of his life."

I knew Trevor was right but it didn't make it any easier.

"Good friends shouldn't desert each other, not by choice, not because something better has come along."

"I know, Mel, but sometimes when you really care about someone you have to learn to let go. That way they stand more chance of coming back to you."

We talked for ages about Hollywell, the horses, Angel and Binny. How much money we needed to raise, how much the Open Day would make. It was

71

so quiet and peaceful it was like another world. I couldn't imagine being anywhere else.

Angel and the foal heard the noise first. They pricked up their ears and stood stock still, straining to see in the dim light. Angel whickered to the foal who anxiously ran behind her out of harm's way.

Trevor was looking straight at me, his fingers folding round the torch. "What was that?" he mouthed.

Goose pimples sprouted on my arms and I didn't know why.

"I was sure I heard footsteps." Trevor was slowly easing back the bolt on the stable door.

We quickly turned off the infra-red heat lamps and waited for a few minutes in the darkness, listening for the slightest noise. What if it was a burglar or a horse thief?

Nothing.

"Honestly, Mel, I heard footsteps, I would bet my life on it."

We switched on the torch and decided to go walkabout, clinging to each other for moral support.

"Maybe we ought to wake the others?" I hissed, shaking like a leaf.

Snowy blinked at us from his stable and Isabella snorted in her special pen. There was no sign of any disturbance. Even so, I had a feeling someone was out there, something wasn't quite right.

Suddenly a dustbin lid clattered from behind the house and a strange black cat shot off with its coat stuck on end.

Relief made me breathless.

"It must be that knock on the head." Trevor jokingly put the blame on me. "You've started hearing things."

The next morning dawned bright with thin rays of yellow sun attempting to dry out the sodden ground. For the first time in days I actually managed to laugh at one of Katie's jokes and sing along to the radio. Katie insisted that Angel found Radio One therapeutic.

Sarah came back from an early morning walk with a buttercup behind her ear and a pen still clutched in her hand. She'd got the worst attack of writer's block and nothing she did would give her the slightest inspiration, not even the banana and salad cream sandwiches which had worked a treat on her last book. James said it was because she'd got too much on her mind what with Danny, the Open Day, and all this business with Angel.

The previous night she'd worked herself up into a terrible stew over Mrs Barrat who was supposed to have rung her about Danny starting his new school. She hadn't done, and when Sarah had contacted her there was no answer.

"There's something wrong, Mel, I just know it."

I must admit, I was inclined to agree.

"Ross, Blake, you finish the morning feeds. Mel, you're coming with me!" Sarah flounced off towards the house, her red hair tumbling loose down her shoulders and her green eyes flashing, which always meant trouble.

Jigsaw was sprawled in the kitchen doorway, dreamily chewing on a bone, which nearly caused Sarah to go flying and made me stub my toe on a box of Hollywell mugs and teapots.

"Well, they've got to be here somewhere." Sarah had lost both her reading glasses and her address book, which was why she'd dragged me into the house after her. "Come on, Mel, you're the practical one, where would I put them?"

I rescued her address book from among the vegetable peelings and torn-up show schedules in the bin liner but there was no sign of her glasses.

"Now come on, let's get hold of Mrs Barrat and find out what's really going on."

I dialled the number for her and she nearly dragged the phone out of its socket pacing back and forth.

"I want to speak to Mrs Barrat now . . . What

74

do you mean she's not there?" Sarah's temper was hitting boiling point. "Why the hell didn't you tell me this sooner?"

Jigsaw suddenly looked worried and started burying his bone in the laundry basket.

"So where is he now?" Sarah sounded murderous.

I crept out and half closed the door behind me, then picked up a screwed-up letter I'd found among the rubbish. The address at the top read: Salthurst Stud, County Clare, Ireland. "Dear Blake . . ."

I couldn't drag my eyes away.

"He's missing!" Sarah blasted through the door minutes later. "He's run away. Danny's gone!" Her whole body was trembling with shock.

"What do you mean? Where? How?" I couldn't believe it.

Apparently Sarah had been talking to Mr Barrat who couldn't take the strain any more. Danny had run away on the first night. Mrs Barrat had refused to tell anyone, especially Sarah. She figured Danny had tried to make his way back to Hollywell but he didn't have any money and she thought he'd soon give up and come back with his tail between his legs. But that had been nearly a week ago.

"Can you believe it?" Sarah screeched. "A nine-year-old boy sleeping rough and she hasn't even contacted the police. What kind of woman is she?"

My head was still reeling with shock. It brought back memories of when we'd first met Danny, how he'd been looking after himself because his mother was staying with her boyfriend. We should never have let her take him.

"Mel, there's a little boy out there completely defenceless. Anything could have happened." Sarah crashed into a chair and buried her head in her hands. "It's all my fault, I should never have agreed . . ."

"Danny's tough," I said. "He's used to fending for himself, if anyone can survive he can." I tried not to let her hear the icy fear in my voice.

"Sarah!" Blake bounded into the kitchen, breathless and as white as a sheet. I'd never seen him so shaken. His hands were trembling.

"What is it? What's happened?"

He leaned against the doorframe gasping for breath. "Quick, it's serious!"

All thoughts of Danny shot out of my head. I'd never seen Blake like this before – he looked as if he'd seen a ghost. Sarah was at the door before I'd even pulled on my boots.

"Blake, wait!"

We dashed out into the stable yard not knowing what to expect. The outside tap was running over and the yard brush was just slung down on the concrete; everywhere looked deserted. It was obvious something terrible must have happened, it could only be one of the horses . . .

"Blake!"

He ran on ahead towards Queenie's old stable where Ross was standing at the door frantically waving for us to be quiet.

That was it, then, the stallion must have died in the night or escaped. It was so quiet you could hear a pin drop, no kicking or wild neighing or marching round and round. I hated myself for suddenly feeling glad it was the stallion and not Queenie, or Snowy or Boris or Jakey – one of the old favourites.

"Ssssh, don't say a word." Ross put a hand on Sarah's shoulder. "One wrong move and it could set off a timebomb."

Blake dragged back the bolt on the stable door and it grated open a few inches at a time. Sunlight flooded in. I could hardly bring myself to look.

I imagined seeing the stallion laid out in the straw or maybe having a fit or a bout of colic but it wasn't anything like that. For the first time in my life I was completely stuck for words.

"I couldn't believe it either," Blake whispered behind me.

Sarah breathed in sharply and her hand flew up to her mouth.

"Trevor wasn't imagining footsteps after all," I murmured.

The bundle of horse rugs fell back to reveal our mystery intruder.

"Danny!" Sarah gasped.

There was no mistaking that tousled brown hair. It was Danny. He'd come back home.

"Well, you could have used the front door like ordinary people instead of frightening the life out of me and Mel." Trevor poked his head round the stable door, loaded up with crisps and chocolate from the village shop. "Gee, Mrs F., he looks awful!"

Danny grinned at us from inside three horse rugs, straw stuck to his hair and streaks of grime down both cheeks. He looked washed out and exhausted, but at least he was alive and in one piece. He also seemed to have made a new friend.

The stallion was standing over Danny, relaxed and happy, nodding his head up and down, every so often nuzzling Danny's neck. He was being so gentle, so inquisitive, his eyes full of tenderness and concern. He was a completely different horse.

"It's a miracle," said Sarah. "Is that the same horse? You know, the one that tried to crush James to death?"

"And charged at Mel." Blake gave me a warm look.

It *was* pretty amazing.

"Where did he come from?" Danny threw his arms round the charcoal-black neck and nearly gave us all palpitations.

"Danny, be careful, you don't know anything about him. He's not all he appears."

"Danny!" Katie pushed past Ross, immediately dropping a box of eggs and a loaf of bread on the brick floor. She screeched so loud I honestly thought the window was going to cave in. "You're back!"

"Here." Sarah shovelled heaps of glucose into a mug of tea and passed it to Danny. "Get that down you, it's good for shock."

"But I'm not in shock." Danny was hugging little Oscar to death.

"A proper breakfast, that's what you need. Now where are those eggs?"

"Where is he?" James rushed in and went sprawling over Jigsaw's bone. "I got here as soon as I could."

"He spent the night with the stallion." Sarah flicked margarine everywhere as she waved the knife around like a baton.

"Now then, my little shrimp, how are you?" James put his hand on Danny's head.

Danny rolled his eyes at Sarah, who was fussing like a mother goose and busily putting the teapot inside the microwave. James chuckled and pulled her back by the hair, plonking the teapot on the table and taking her in his arms. It was only then that I noticed her T-shirt was on inside out and back to front and her pump laces were both undone.

"Oh James, what are we going to do?"

Danny's eyes grew to the size of tractor wheels as we told him about Angel, the foal and Blackie.

"But he's so gentle," he said.

Mrs Mac arrived carrying a bundle of Hollywell sweatshirts and dropped the whole lot as soon as she saw Danny. "Good heavens, he's as thin as a blade," she said, slapping a pudgy hand on his forehead.

"It seems to me," James said, after listening to the whole story, "that that mad cracker of a horse has finally found a friend." It was really weird how the stallion had taken to Danny.

"Maybe," Katie said, stuffing her mouth with bread and strawberry jam, "it was because Danny went in there thinking it was Queenie and he didn't have any nerves."

"Possibly," Blake joined in. "Horses can smell fear a mile off."

I avoided his eyes and dug the dirt out of my finger-nails. "Should somebody contact Danny's mother?" I blurted out.

I might as well have dropped a bombshell if Danny's face was anything to go by.

"I'm not going back," he quivered. "I'm not, I'm not, not ever!" He bolted upstairs and slammed his bedroom door.

"I'd better take these up." Katie fetched a bag full to bursting from the pantry. It contained all the odds and ends that reminded her of Danny. "I didn't think he was ever coming back."

Chapter Eight

The rest of the day zoomed by. Danny helped bottle-feed the foal, who insisted on sniffing his hair and all his clothes. Danny said she was gorgeous and what were we going to call her. We couldn't keep saying "the foal".

"I think it's rather up to Binny," I said. "After all, they will be going back to her place when they're both strong enough."

Katie's face blackened and I knew she'd been harbouring hopes of them staying at Hollywell. She'd been spouting on about how to train foals and Sarah had caught her reading a youngstock handbook under the duvet at one o'clock in the morning.

"There's no way an old lady can look after her," she snapped. "It's not fair."

The Open Day was looming and there was still a mountain of things to do. I took my antibiotic tablet, put on an extra sweatshirt and threw myself into organizing the photograph displays – it helped take my mind off Blake and how ill I was starting to feel. I was just sorting through some before-and-after pictures of Jakey, an old piebald cob we had rescued, when James came into the office looking exhausted. He'd just been examining Blackie and giving him a tetanus and multi-vitamin injection.

"I don't know what's happened to that horse," he said, "but it's a transformation."

We'd had a Hollywell meeting earlier and all agreed that as soon as Blackie was strong enough he'd have to be gelded. We couldn't cope with a stallion, not with all the mares that were at the sanctuary. Sarah had phoned the blacksmith to have his feet trimmed and James was going to treat him for lice. In the meantime Danny was practically living in his stable.

"Mel, I really think we need to talk." Blake came in, still in his jodhpurs and riding boots, his hair glistening with sweat. "We can't go on like this."

I thumped some Blu-Tac on the display stand and marched off to Angel's stable. I knew if we started talking I'd lose my temper and I didn't want to say anything I'd regret.

Katie was leading the foal round in the head-collar slip Binny had bought, and was about to give her a feed. She tried to convince me that her mane had grown at least two centimetres, but I wasn't really listening. I was too busy thinking about the crumpled letter in my pocket and all the things Blake hadn't told me.

Ross came out of the house looking ponderous, with Jigsaw diving around his ankles. "Mrs Barrat's on the phone," he whispered. "Something's up, I just know it. Sarah's doodling like mad on the telephone pad."

At least while Mrs Barrat was on the phone we weren't being plagued by reporters. News had got out about the capture of the Black Beast and it was causing a sensation right through the country. Some people were still insisting it was a big cat or a llama and we'd even had sightseers gathering at the bottom of the drive in the hope of seeing something.

Sarah appeared looking exhausted, and cursed when she saw that James's car had gone. "Blast, just when I really needed to speak to him."

"You've missed him by seconds," I said. "He's gone back to the surgery."

We all tried to find out what Mrs Barrat had said but for some reason Sarah was being unusually mysterious. "I've got to speak to James first," she said. "It's something very important." She dived into her car and shot out of the drive.

Danny was sitting on an upturned bucket in Blackie's stable, telling him his life story and sharing a cup of tea. I listened outside the door for a few minutes and then sloped off with a lump in my throat. For a nine-year-old boy he'd been through too much. But then so had the stallion. Sarah was intent on giving Danny a lecture on running away, as soon as he was back to his normal self. It was a really stupid and dangerous thing to do, and running away from your problems never solves anything, it usually just makes everything a hundred times worse.

"Hey, look at this." Trevor nudged my arm and we turned to where Danny was leading the stallion into the main yard. Both of them were moving really slowly and hesitantly, finding their feet. Danny only came up to the stallion's shoulder. He'd looped a piece of baling string through the headcollar and was clinging on with both hands, looking at Blackie. I don't think Blackie planned on going anywhere – he was glued to Danny's side.

Jigsaw barked and waved his paw and Snowy dropped the mouthful of hay he was eating. Even Isabella stopped rooting, and stood and stared with her beady eyes.

But it was Angel that Blackie was really interested in. As soon as he heard her whinny he dashed over to the stable, plunging his head over the top and burying his nose in her cream mane. He sniffed her all over, from the tips of her ears to the tip of her nose, and then it was the foal's turn.

She was scrabbling up the door determined not to be left out. They were the perfect family unit and it was so obvious that Angel and Blackie were in love.

"Isn't it great?" Danny grinned, patting the thick black neck.

"It's straight out of a Barbara Cartland novel." Mrs Mac had appeared from the office with tears running down her cheeks. "I wish Sarah was here to see this."

"I honestly thought he'd have to be put down." Ross stopped Jigsaw from getting too close.

"He's a real looker." Blake took in the fine Arab lines and beautiful chest and hindquarters.

We could see his beauty now he was out in daylight. All the other mares seemed to be thinking the same thing because I'd never seen so many heads pop up over the stable doors. They were queuing up at the field gate. Snowy was glaring at Blackie as if a Hollywood film star had just walked into the yard.

"He's only got eyes for Angel." Katie looked really dreamy.

I ran and fetched a Jammy Dodger from the tack room and broke it in half for Angel and Blackie.

"Isn't he just the best horse you've ever seen?" Danny was patting Blackie's shoulder and pulling burrs out of his long tangled mane. "He's going to stay here for ever and ever. He's never going to be ill-treated again."

Sarah came back an hour later saying that she hadn't managed to track down James. He was out at a racing stables and he wasn't answering his phone.

"So what's the big mystery?" Ross couldn't wait any longer. "We've never kept secrets before, you can't tell us that nothing's happened."

Sarah put some frozen pizzas in the oven for lunch and turned round to face us.

"OK, I get your point. I'll tell you what I know, which isn't much."

"And Danny as well." Ross put his hand on top of Danny's head. "He's part of the family, too."

We all sat down with cheese and pineapple pizza and Sarah started to open up.

"It's not just your mother, Danny, there's something else."

Apparently a Mr Parker had been in touch with Sarah early that morning. Blackie's story had leaked to all the national papers and a couple of them had been prompting people to come forward with any information about the Black Beast. Mr Parker hadn't minced his words. He'd got our number from the RSPCA and he had a very serious claim. He insisted that a year ago his black horse was stolen from its field near a main road. He was saying that Blackie was his and he wanted him back.

"Of course he's got to prove it first." Sarah was trying not to sound worried, but it was hopeless. Her knife and fork clattered against her plate. "I'll have to be honest though." She pushed the pizza away. "It doesn't look good."

If Mr Parker could prove that Blackie was his horse and he had the right facilities to keep him then there was nothing we could do. We'd have to let him go.

"He knows his age and size," Sarah said. "And I checked with the chief constable – there was a horse reported missing at his address a year ago."

"Oh great, that says it all, doesn't it?" Ross screwed up the kitchen roll in frustration.

"There was one other thing though," Sarah said. "His horse has a scar on his neck underneath his mane – something to do with a road accident."

"So does Blackie." Danny's voice was on the verge of desperation. "I saw it this morning."

"Do you really think Mr Parker will take Blackie away?" Katie had followed me into one of the fields where I was frantically pulling up some ragwort. It seemed almost symbolic that if I could rid the fields of every trace of poisonous plants it might somehow clear all the bad stuff from our lives. And Heaven knows, there was enough of it.

Mrs Barrat was due to arrive tomorrow morning. Apparently she had something very important to discuss with Danny, but Sarah refused to tell us any more. She said she had to talk to James first.

Danny was trying very hard to put on a brave face. He insisted on dousing Blackie with the lice powder all by himself even though he ended up more de-loused than Blackie. Trevor said at least nobody could accuse him of having nits and Sarah sent him straight upstairs to have a bath. I never realized that you could actually see the lice moving around in the coat and it was no wonder that poor Blackie was scratching himself silly.

Poor Danny. Two blows in as many minutes and he was walking around as if someone had hit him with a sledgehammer.

"It'll break his heart if Blackie goes." Katie had never sounded more serious.

"I know," I said. "But what can we do?"

They say trouble always comes in threes but none of us was prepared for what happened next. In hindsight we should have known – it was so obvious.

*

That evening we decided to make the most of the dry weather and have a barbecue. Ross kindly told me I looked like something the cat had dragged in, and Blake went off to see Mr Sullivan about his sponsorship deal and no doubt to inform him that his new address would be in Ireland.

We organized the night rota for feeding the foal. Katie and Danny were to do the two o'clock shift and Trevor and I the four o'clock. Sarah said it was good to give Danny some extra responsibility and it would take his mind off Blackie. If they had any trouble they were to wake me at once. As my bedroom was nearest the stables I was sure to hear them anyway.

I threw some chicken legs on the barbecue and took another antibiotic tablet. Binny had arrived and was fussing Angel to death and rearranging her straw bed and her hay net. Sarah was wandering around with a bottle of barbecue sauce and the synopsis for her next book.

"Mel, what on earth's the matter? You look awful!" Sarah said.

I didn't remember much after that. I was completely knocked out, and I hit the pillow like a ton of bricks.

*

"Mel, Mel, wake up!" It was gone four o'clock when Trevor shook my shoulders until my teeth rattled.

"What is it? Leave me alone. I want to sleep."

"Melanie!" There was something in Trevor's voice which suddenly made me sit bolt upright and force my eyes open.

"It's Danny. And Katie. They've gone. They've taken Blackie!"

Chapter Nine

"But they can't have run away. They're not that stupid."

Blackie's stable door was swinging open. Empty.

"Maybe they've just taken him for a walk. It's more than possible."

"Look at this." Ross picked up a pink envelope from inside the manger and ripped it open.

Inside was a note in Katie's handwriting: "We didn't have a choice. Don't try to find us. We'll be in touch."

"It's all my fault." Sarah broke down in tears. "I should have told him. If only I'd said something this would never have happened."

We regrouped in the kitchen feeling completely shell-shocked. This was the last thing any of us had expected.

Sarah started to explain how Mrs Barrat wanted her and James to take Danny on full-time, to foster him.

"I didn't want to say anything until I'd spoken to James. I didn't want to build up Danny's hopes."

"And now it's too late." Ross clenched his fists.

"Listen, guys, they can't have got that far." Blake stood up, pushing back his dark hair, trying to think logically. "Surely somebody's seen two kids and a black stallion, they're hardly inconspicuous, and they've only been gone a couple of hours."

We dived into the car, not even aware that it was only 5 o'clock in the morning. All our thoughts were on finding Danny and Katie. Trevor stayed behind at Hollywell in case they came back.

"And Blackie. When all's said and done," Sarah said, "he's still a wild horse, he could turn at any time."

The village High Street was completely deserted, not a person in sight.

"It's my guess they'll have headed for the bridle-paths." Blake was scanning all around him. "Danny wouldn't have wanted to take Blackie on the roads. Not once the traffic starts to build up."

"They could be anywhere," I said, feeling helpless.

"We've got to think positive." Ross squeezed my hand. "It's going to be all right."

"Knowing Danny, he won't change his mind," I said. "He's got nothing to lose."

The early morning mist was starting to lift and

a clear blue sky shone through. It was going to be hot.

We checked out two of the local bridlepaths and farm tracks where we went riding, but there was nothing, not even a fresh hoofprint.

"Mel, are you sure they didn't say anything to you, any clue, anything that might give us an ink-ling?" Sarah slipped the car into fourth gear and we headed for the next village.

"I can't think," I almost shrieked. "I've gone blank."

"Here, stop! There's a milk float!" Ross dived out of the car and held up a milkman coming out of someone's front gate.

"Have you seen a young boy and girl and a black horse?"

It was hopeless. Nobody had seen anything. We stopped three people leaving early for work and one woman walking her dog. They all looked vague and shook their heads. A paperboy thought he'd seen someone riding a black horse but it turned out to be a riding instructor from the local livery stables. She hadn't seen anything either.

"It's a wild goose chase." Blake got back in the car and yanked the seatbelt across his front. "I can't believe nobody's seen them."

We scoured the next four villages, all the back lanes and tracks for miles around. Not a glimpse.

"I think we ought to go back home." Blake was the first to say what we were all thinking.

"Maybe they've come back." Ross sounded hopeful.

Our spirits were low as we made our way home, and it was already half past seven by the time we reached Hollywell.

"The phone's not rung once." Trevor was in the kitchen with Jigsaw, trying to stay calm.

"There's only one thing for it." Sarah collapsed in the armchair looking exhausted. "We'll have to contact the police."

"We'll do everything we can." The police officer stood in our kitchen taking down all the details including Katie's note. "I'll put out an alert. We'll pick them up in no time. The best thing is not to worry."

Sarah looked more drained than I'd ever seen her. "They're only kids, officer, they don't know what they're doing."

I thought back to what Danny had told me about his trip up from Brighton. How he'd thumbed lifts from lorry drivers and devoured half-eaten burgers from waste bins outside transport cafés. It was no way for a child to live.

"Katie's never done anything like this before." Sarah told the officer.

"Danny will look after her," I said. "She's his best friend. She wanted to stick by him."

"Don't worry, love, we'll find them."

Despite the crisis, life had to go on. Trevor and I went out to feed the horses and the foal. Sarah rang round all of Katie's friends to see if they knew anything. Blake and Ross went out for another search.

"I feel so useless," I said, picking bits of straw out of Angel's mane while Trevor finished feeding the foal. "I should have known something like this would happen."

"Eh, come on, now don't be so daft," Trevor said. "You can't go blaming yourself. It's nobody's fault. We've just got to cope. That's what life's about – coping."

He gave me a massive hug, which felt like being squeezed by a grizzly bear and I instantly felt better. "You now, sometimes, Trevor, I don't know how I managed without you."

By eleven o'clock there was still no news and we hadn't heard from Blake or Ross. Sarah was listless with anxiety and Jigsaw kept moping around with his tail between his legs. Trevor and I finished off Angel's packet of Jammy Dodgers which had gone soggy and made some coffee which was too strong.

"It's Binny." Sarah looked through the window. "I wonder what she's doing here?"

"It's no good, Sarah, I'm just not happy with the situation." Binny marched into the kitchen very much like the first time we'd met her. She was bristling with anger and took us all off guard.

"Angel's my baby. It should be me who's looking after her. But since she's been here, you lot have just taken over. It's as if I don't exist." Binny stood, trembling, wringing her hands together. Everything had been bottled up and now suddenly, came pouring out.

We all just stood and gaped. I knew Binny was really fussy about how we were looking after Angel, but we were the ones who were sitting up night after night feeding the foal until we couldn't think straight with exhaustion. It was Hollywell that up to now had paid for all Angel's treatment and the foal milk.

Sarah was livid. She slung down the tea towel and looked Binny straight in the eye. "How dare you march into my house and talk to us like that? Angel might be the only thing on your mind but we've got two children missing. At the moment we don't know where they are, what's happened, they've been out all night . . ." Sarah's voice caught in her throat with emotion. She turned away and stared out of the window, her whole body shaking.

"I'm so sorry, I didn't realize, I had no idea." Binny gave a little sob and stumbled for the door. Trevor went out after her, keen to check that she was all right.

I went across to put my arms round Sarah. She hadn't meant what she'd said, she was just so upset.

"Oh, Mel, I should never have told Danny about Mr Parker. What kind of mother am I?"

"The best," I said, hugging her as hard as I could. "Without you there wouldn't be a Holly-well, we wouldn't be a family, Danny would still be with that awful woman. It's going to be all right, I know it is."

Trevor came back in, followed by two officers in uniform. "It's the police," he said. "They want to ask more questions."

Mrs Barrat arrived in the afternoon with her husband, but surprisingly they took the whole ordeal in their stride. I quickly worked out that Mrs Barrat was keen to keep on Sarah's good side. They both wanted Sarah to have Danny while they moved to Scotland. Mr Barrat had been offered a promotion with a new executive car. There would be loads of functions, travelling abroad. Danny wouldn't fit in.

It sounded to me as if the novelty of having Danny had quickly worn off. Mr Barrat just seemed eager to get rid of the whole problem. He didn't seem to be quite the wimp I first thought.

"Now Sarah, you sit down, dear, and I'll make you a cup of tea." Mrs Barrat was trying so hard to be nice it was almost funny. She didn't know what to make of the pots piled in the sink or Oscar's half-eaten food or the foal's bottles sitting next to the dirty mugs ready for washing. "It's so nice to be in the country." She gritted her teeth.

She wasn't a bit worried about Danny and Katie. "They'll turn up when they're hungry."

Ross and Blake came back looking defeated and Sarah was a lot better since James had managed to call round in the afternoon. He'd been a hundred miles away vetting some pigs and he didn't have a clue what was going on.

The only phone call we had all day was from Mrs Mac to say that Rocky had been located and he'd just arrived in London. He'd be at Hollywell to officially open the Gala Day.

At the moment, that seemed a million miles away. But James and Sarah said we couldn't cancel; too many arrangements had been made. The show must go on.

It seemed incredible that two children and a horse could completely disappear like this. The whole of the local police force was out looking for them and still hadn't found a thing.

In the end I decided to go for a walk outside. The Barrats were driving me mad and Sarah had decided to start spring cleaning even though it was July.

It was a cool moist evening and I went right round all the stables and then switched the light on in the tack room and sat down.

"Is the Wicked Witch of the West getting too much for you?" Blake poked his head round the door and grinned at me.

I looked down and felt like bursting into tears.

"Here, I think you dropped something." Blake put the crumpled letter from Ireland in my lap and stood back and watched me.

My eyes were welling up. "You could have told me," I said. "I deserved to know the full story."

"Well, you hardly gave me much of a chance, did you?" Blake came and sat down beside me. I could smell his aftershave.

"That's the trouble with you, Blake, you're always so distant and mysterious. How can we be close when sometimes I don't think I even know you?"

He didn't say anything. He just stared ahead.

I opened out the letter and reread the scrawly handwriting. It was from a woman called Tina who had helped Blake enormously when he first started out as a show-jumper. He owed her a lot. She was writing to tell him that she had broken her back in a riding accident. The bank was threatening to close her down, and she had twenty horses and nobody to show-jump them. She really needed Blake to help her out.

"You will write, won't you?" I was having to bite on my lower lip to keep back the tears.

"Oh, Mel." Blake grabbed hold of me and I buried my head in his neck, feeling the warmth of his skin. I felt better than I had done in days. I didn't want him ever to let me go.

"Anyway, there's something I haven't told you." He gently kissed my forehead and held me closer. "I'm not—"

The door blasted open. Trevor loomed in the doorway, urgency written all over his face.

"They've found them!" he yelled. "They're both safe, but they've lost the stallion!"

Chapter Ten

"It's all right, Danny, you're not in trouble, nobody's going to shout at you."

Danny and Katie clambered out of the police car looking scared and bewildered. I never thought I'd be so pleased to see my little sister. "I thought you were a goner." I ruffled the top of her hair.

"You've got to find Blackie." Danny could think of nothing else. "He's all by himself, anything could happen."

Gradually, over Mrs Mac's apple crumble and extra thick chocolate cake, the whole story came out.

A policewoman took down notes in her black book and gently urged Danny for more details. There was a policeman with her who'd been driving the car and he stood and listened. Mr and Mrs Barrat had gone into the sitting-room out of the way because Danny had freaked out as soon as he saw them. If the policeman hadn't been standing near the door I think he would have bolted.

"So we hid out in the wood behind our old house." Danny carried on his story. "And then Blackie got restless, he wouldn't stand still."

"So we decided to head for the road and keep to the grass verge," Katie took over. "We were going to go to Birmingham and join the circus. It was my idea, I thought we'd be safe there."

"Katie, how could you be so irresponsible?" Sarah was pacing up and down, about to erupt, but the policewoman urged her to be quiet.

"So what happened next, Danny?"

They'd been picked up by a patrol car outside a telephone box. They'd been trying to ring Hollywell but the phone was out of order. Thank God the police car came along when it did.

"We were going along the road," Danny said, "when this car slowed down and these lads started shouting and jeering. They said they wanted a ride on Blackie and then they . . ."

"They got out of the car and tried to take Blackie," mumbled Katie. "Two of them got hold of his neck and one of them pushed Danny to the ground. He's got a big bruise on his back to prove it."

"Blackie went berserk," Danny murmured. "He charged at them until they were terrified and then ran off. We thought he'd come back but he didn't.

He just disappeared. That's when we decided to ring home."

"And this was how long ago?" The police-woman jotted down more notes.

"You've got to save him, Mrs F., he's scared, he could do anything."

"It's all right, sonny," the policeman said, "we'll do our best. He's bound to turn up somewhere, they always do." Right on cue his bleeper went off and he spoke into the special mobile radio. I could actually see his face turn a pale shade of grey.

"I think we've located him," he said in a grave voice. "There's a horse loose on the motorway galloping down the central divide. He's black and apparently completely wild."

"That's him!" Danny leapt up. "That's Blackie!"

"There's something I've not told the young lad," the policeman whispered to Sarah outside and I could just hear their conversation. "The horse has gone stark raving bonkers. He's jumped two cars and already caused a pile-up. They've called in a vet. He might have to be . . ."

"No, not that, not if we can get to him first." Sarah was shaking with emotion.

Blake was already unlocking the car.

"Come on, gang." Sarah dragged open the door. "We've got a horse to catch!"

The police siren wailed out ahead of us and

I clung to the seat as Sarah pumped at the accelerator.

"Dip the lights." Blake reached over and fiddled with the switch but it was stuck on full beam. Cars were tooting like mad at us but we hardly noticed.

"I know a short cut." Sarah swung round a corner practically on two wheels and we roared down a narrow lane.

"Sarah, I don't know whether this was a good idea."

"Of course it is." She crashed the gears. "I know what I'm doing."

We'd lost all sight of the police car and I had no idea how far we were from the motorway.

"Turn right here." Ross banged on the indicator and we went hurtling along what looked like a disused airfield.

"I should have brought my flying hat," Ross joked but none of us were in the mood for laughter. Somewhere Blackie was running wild and we had to save him.

"He won't trust anyone," Danny said, "he'll just keep running."

We flew over a concrete mound and Ross said he thought we'd lost the exhaust. We didn't have to look, we could hear, it sounded as if the whole rear end of the car had collapsed.

"Just keep going," Blake said.

We came out at a criss-cross of junctions and Sarah didn't hesitate for a second.

"I hope she knows what she's doing," Katie whispered, clinging on to my arm. I could feel my watch strap pressing into my flesh under her fingers. Time was short, and each passing minute could mean the end.

Ross wound down the window to listen to the exhaust, or lack of it, and a sharp blast of air blew Sarah's hair right across her face.

"Good one, Ross, what are you trying to do, kill us all?"

We charged on at full pelt.

"There it is!" Sarah eventually yelled. "The motorway!"

We screeched to a halt on top of a flyover to get our bearings. We knew we were in the right place because a crowd of people had got out of their cars and were craning to see what was going on.

"Make way, make way." Ross pushed past them all. "We're from the police, Special Branch."

What we saw brought us all up short. There was Blackie, a dark speck, heading towards us, darting from one lane of traffic to another, sliding, careering all over, squeezing past on the hard shoulder, completely demented.

"He's flipped his lid," Danny said in a small voice. "We'll never catch him now."

All the traffic in both directions had slithered to a halt and men were getting out and waving their arms.

"Never say never," Sarah muttered.

"We've got to do something." Ross stood and stared.

It was no good us going down on to the motorway. There was so much traffic we'd never get near him.

"Oh no." Blake drew in his breath. "They've brought in the army."

A helicopter suddenly appeared, hovering towards us, a man leaning out with what looked like a rifle. Some people on the flyover started cheering and one woman said Blackie had demolished three cars and caused a tailback for ten miles.

"For goodness' sake, have a heart," Sarah snapped. "Can't you see the poor horse is terrified?"

The helicopter was trying to shunt Blackie off the fast lane on to the slip road where we could just see a barricade and police officers.

Blackie saw them too. His mane and tail flew up in the breeze from the propellers and he darted and swivelled round, his hind legs at one instant dipping right underneath him.

"He's going up the bank," Danny screamed. "He'll never make it, it's too steep!"

He was scrabbling up the bank in sheer terror,

107

his whole body lunging forward in a series of cat leaps.

"If he falls he'll break his neck."

"It's just like on television, isn't it, dear?" One woman turned to an older one. It was probably more excitement than she'd had in the last twenty years.

"Way to go, Blackie!" Danny was pumping the air with his fist.

"He's done it, look, he's reached the top!"

"Run, Blackie, run!" Danny's eyes were filled with tears.

"Come on," Sarah yelled. "We've got to get to him first!"

We belted across a roundabout, not even bothering to check for oncoming traffic. Everything was pandemonium, with police cars going in all directions.

"He's gone that way!" A man walking his dog was pointing like mad.

"Poor Blackie, he must feel like a hunted animal," I said, almost sick with pity.

"Come on, Blackie, where are you?" Sarah drove down a dual carriageway leading into the town centre. Two police cars overtook us, burning rubber.

"There's Trevor, in the back of that last car," said Ross.

We set off in pursuit.

"Sarah, I hate to say this but you've just gone through a red light."

"Not now, Blake, I'm concentrating."

Trees and telegraph poles were whipping past in a blur.

"Turn right, they've all gone right," Ross yanked the indicator so hard it dropped off.

We were heading into a built-up estate. Anything could happen now: Blackie could knock somebody down. What if he ran into a child?

People were racing out to their gates, lights were going on right down the streets. Two police cars had loudspeakers and were telling everybody to stay inside, there was a wild horse running loose and potentially lethal: "Under no circumstances step into the road."

All the activity was coming from a road signposted as a dead end.

"Oh no," Ross groaned, "they've got him cornered."

We turned down the road not knowing what to expect. The first thing we saw was Trevor arguing with a police officer. And then we spotted Blackie, drenched through with sweat, trembling uncontrollably, cornered in someone's front garden, snapping his teeth and snaking his neck at anybody who dared go near.

The police officer nearest Trevor loaded a rifle.

"No!" Sarah yelled, bursting out of the car, the engine still running.

"I can catch him," Danny pleaded with the police officers. "I know I can, just give me five minutes. He's my friend."

Danny edged towards the stallion, all the time talking and holding out his hand.

"If anything happens to that young lad . . ." One of the officers looked terrified.

"It won't, he knows what he's doing." Sarah didn't take her eyes off Danny's back.

"You shouldn't have run away," Danny gabbled on to the stallion, "you've brought this all on yourself. I know those lads scared you and then all those cars, but you can't keep running away. I've learnt that. It doesn't solve anything. It doesn't make things better."

The stallion snorted and pawed the ground. He was listening, he'd recognized Danny and that was a start.

"You can have a good life at Hollywell," Danny said. "I didn't mean it when I told you about Mr Parker, that's all sorted now," Danny lied. "He's not going to take you away."

A huge great lump caught in my throat. Of course the stallion didn't know what Danny was saying. He was responding to the tone of his voice, like all horses do.

"I'll just stroke your neck like that and we can be friends again." Danny reached up to the huge black crest. "It's all right, nobody's going to hurt you, I'm just going to slip on this headcollar, like we did in the stable."

The stallion lolled his head, utterly defeated, trusting Danny to look after him.

"What a hero," a police officer whispered to Sarah. "He must have nerves of steel."

"No," Sarah said, swallowing back the tears, "he knows what it's like to be totally alone with nobody on your side. It's not very nice."

The stallion edged forward across to Trevor and the rest of us, sore-footed from all that galloping and still trembling, but not quite as much.

"You poor old soul." I reached up my hand to his flared nostrils and Sarah fetched a rug from the boot of the car and laid it over his back to stop him getting cold.

"I think," Sarah said, putting an arm round my shoulders, "this is when we fetch the horsebox, don't you?"

"Hip, hip – hooray!" Sarah and James raised their glasses.

"Hip, hip," Katie shouted.

"Hooray!" we all yelled.

We were all sitting in the kitchen toasting Danny and demolishing the remains of a congratulations cake. Jigsaw was under the table crunching on some icing and Danny was trying to pick a model of a horse off the top of the cake but it was stuck in the jam.

"I can't believe it," Katie said for the hundredth time. "It's the best happy ending we've ever had."

"It's purrfect," Ross drawled, stroking Oscar who was flicking a pickled onion across the tablecloth.

It really was the perfect ending to a traumatic week. It was seven o'clock the night after we'd rescued Blackie and since that moment it had been like a whirlwind. Blackie and Danny had been on television and in the local paper. Luckily nobody had been injured on the motorway and there was just the headache of sorting out the insurance. Mr and Mrs Barrat had set off for Scotland, and Danny was still trying to take in the news that he could stay at Hollywell. James and Sarah were even talking about adopting him.

"It's just the best." Katie gobbled a sausage on a stick. We hadn't heard any more from Mr Parker so we presumed he'd changed his mind or it had all been a hoax in the first place.

"Here's to Blackie and Danny," said James.

"And the Open Day!" Danny added and we all groaned out loud.

In precisely sixteen hours we'd be welcoming the first flood of Hollywell fans through the gates. My stomach was curling up at the thought of it. And we still had half a dozen horses to wash tomorrow morning. We'd been flat out all day making the final arrangements.

We'd just got the caravan and loudspeaker set up when Rocky telephoned to say he'd be there to cut the red ribbon, wild horses wouldn't keep him away.

"He's obviously not heard about Blackie," Ross joked.

Everything was ready and just waiting for the morning. The only fly in the ointment was the lack of burger bar, but I guess we couldn't have everything. If it all went to plan we could make enough for next winter's hay bill and more besides.

"I wonder how many people will turn up?" said Katie.

"Thousands," Danny munched and we all laughed out loud.

"Who's this?" Blake fiddled with the curtain and suddenly became unusually quiet. "It looks like we've got company."

The blue pick-up truck pulled into the yard and

we all piled outside. We didn't suspect anything out of the ordinary; I thought it was someone wanting to leave a horse with us. Since Hollywell Stables had become famous we'd received calls every week about ponies needing good homes and in the main we managed to foster them out to loving families.

"I want to see the guv'nor." A man with slate-grey hair and big dealer boots with steel caps stood in the yard looking round as if he owned the place. There was a girl with him but she stayed in the truck, almost slithering down the seat so we didn't spot her. Then again, that was quite normal – people often got embarrassed when they came to ask for a home for their horse, especially if they didn't have any money, which was usually the reason they were turning to us.

But I didn't like this man – there was something unsettling about him. They say first impressions are usually the right ones and from the moment he turned and faced me I felt myself cringe with unease.

"Yes, I'm the guv'nor, as you call it." Sarah bristled with distaste.

"Good." The man quickly rubbed a hand on his trouser leg and held it out to Sarah. "The name's Parker," he said, "Dave Parker. I've come for my horse."

We all looked devastated. We should have known, suspected at least, but as it was, it hit us like a bolt out of the blue. Trevor scratched his head looking gormless and Ross nearly choked on a sausage roll.

"Oh," Sarah said, "I see."

"So come on, where is he, then? Look sharp."

He was horrible. He was probably the worst person we could ever have chosen to take Blackie. He wouldn't know a sensitive thought if it jumped up and bit him on the nose.

"What are we going to do?" I whispered to Blake as Mr Parker blundered off to look in the nearest stable. Sarah was frantic. Ross had his jaw set and Blake had a nervous twitch in his cheek.

"Do something," I hissed, not having a clue what to suggest.

Thanks heavens Danny and Katie were in the house. James came out sizing up the situation and immediately taking charge. "There's no way that horse is to be moved for a few days. He's had too big a shock."

"That's right," Sarah said, "he's not going anywhere."

"Aye, but you can let me have a look at him. Check that he's the right horse. That's not so much to ask."

Sarah pursed her lips, which always meant she

was unsure, and then finally agreed to lead him round to Blackie's stable. With any luck he might have got it wrong.

"Yeah, and pigs might fly," Ross whispered behind me.

"He's always been a wild one, you know, I always said he was soft in the head." Mr Parker marched along at Sarah's side rubbing his hands together and gawping at everything with his tight piggy eyes.

"He smells more fishy than a fish and chip shop." Blake bent closer. "He's a conman, Mel, I would bet my life on it."

"Yeah, so how does he know so much about Blackie?" Blake didn't have an answer.

Mr Parker shoved his head over the door and his eye lit up like headlights. "That's him all right, the big black 'un, we call him Jet."

I felt sick to the bottom of my stomach.

I was just about to turn away when Blackie lunged at the door, snapping his teeth inches from Mr Parker's face. He was going berserk.

"Shut him in," Sarah yelled, "he's going crazy!"

All we could hear was lashing hooves and splintering wood. I honestly thought he was going to break down the door.

"Get away from him!" James yelled at Mr Parker who was still standing in a daze. Sarah grabbed him by the arm and dragged him away before Blackie went completely hysterical.

The girl had got out of the truck and stood staring at us. She had streaks of tears down both cheeks and she was trembling like a leaf. "Satisfied now? Satisfied at what you've done to an innocent animal? He was as sweet as pie when we first got him . . ." she cried.

"Rachel, I'm warning you."

"You've done this, you and your filthy temper. I hate you!" She was crying, her face bright red, no older than her late teens.

"Rachel, I've told you to keep your mouth shut."

"You don't scare me any more. I've had it with you, you disgust me."

She was gasping for breath and James moved forward to try and calm her down. Blake, Ross and I stood with our mouths open gaping.

"Don't you see, it was Dad!" she flared up again. "He took him to the moor and he dumped him. He was *my* horse but he didn't care. Now he thinks Jet's worth a fortune, he's only interested in lining his own pockets."

She broke down sobbing and James led her back to the truck with one arm round her shoulders. The truth was finally out. It was Mr Parker who had abandoned Blackie.

"Get off my property." Sarah turned on him

with pure loathing. "You miserable worm of a man. If I ever see you again I won't be responsible for my actions."

The truck rattled down the drive and disappeared from sight. Blackie was ours, nobody would ever threaten to take him away again.

We all stood gathering our wits, taking in what we'd just heard. It was the last piece of the jigsaw to fall into place.

"Mel, Sarah!" Katie and Danny came running up from the main yard, totally oblivious to what had happened, still thinking it was just a man offering us a horse.

"It's Angel," Katie shrieked, still on cloud nine from the party. "Her milk's come down, she's feeding the foal!"

Chapter Eleven

The alarm clock went off at precisely two minutes past five and from that moment onwards it was complete bedlam.

"I told you we should have washed their tails last night." Ross was storming round the house, eating toast and complaining that nothing ever went to plan.

Katie charged in to announce there was no more horse shampoo and could she use washing-up liquid instead? Sarah threw her some of her own apple blossom conditioner and howled when she saw the dirty footprints all over the floor.

James had taken the whole day off work and was clearing the breakfast dishes. Sarah said she hoped he'd buy her a dishwasher when they were married, and started squirting around with air freshener until none of us could breathe and my eyes were stinging.

"For Heaven's sake, Sarah, they're visiting the stables, not the house."

One of the first tasks of the day was to clean up

the horses who were going to appear in the parade. As usual Snowy was plastered in stable stains and his pure white coat had turned a dirty green. Walter had escaped into the greenhouse and was dreamily chewing on a cucumber plant and Big Boris had just slung his bucket over the stable door in a temper because somebody had forgotten his extra oats.

"We'll never be ready in time," Katie whined, gushing a river of hot water over Snowy's back and scrubbing like mad. Danny was flicking soap out of his own ears, never mind Snowy's.

I went across to Angel who was happily chewing at her hay and feeding the foal. We'd moved Blackie next door to her and I was convinced if he strained his neck much more to look at her he'd end up having to wear a surgical collar.

"A small price to pay for true love." Blake put down the wheelbarrow and stood and gazed at them.

I dived into the tack room feeling emotional because Blake was leaving straight after the Open Day. He'd been shut in his room for hours last night, no doubt packing his things. Life was never completely perfect.

"Mel, where's the sweat scraper? And all the towels are wet!" Katie suddenly realized she'd used Sarah's brand-new peach bath towel and turned beetroot, especially when Sarah shouted she was just popping into the shower.

We scrubbed and toiled for what seemed hours and ended up with aching muscles and pricked fingers from plaiting up manes. Katie still couldn't get her plaits any smaller than gold balls and I had to admit it wasn't as easy as it looked.

By eight o'clock a pale pink sun was poking through a reddish tinted sky casting the whole horizon in a warm glow.

"It's going to be a scorcher." James came out with pint mugs of tea and piles of Jammy Dodgers. Since Angel had arrived we'd been living off them.

"We're on course," I said. "The craft stalls should be arriving any minute."

Blake decided to put out a few more straw bales round the yard for people to sit on and Katie rooted out another couple of "No Smoking" signs – you could never be too careful. Ross was getting all tied up in bunting and streamers and Sarah had come to the rescue with the garden shears. "Has anybody seen that peach towel?"

Twenty past eight and Mrs Mac swept in with her team of WI helpers, and stalls selling every-thing from cakes, plants, home-made wine and bric-à-brac, and a tombola. It was starting to feel like a real Gala Day.

"That was Binny on the phone." James came

out of the house carrying all the clean headcollars. "She's asked us if she could come over – she sounded really edgy."

Sarah immediately dropped a plastic flag she was tying to the outside tap and stepped back into a half-empty haynet. "I think," she said jumpily, "this is when I start eating humble pie."

"By the bucketload." James gave her a meaningful look.

Binny marched across the yard looking as if she'd just been dragged through a hedge or at best had a bad night. Sarah had contacted her straight away about Angel now having enough milk to feed the foal, but Binny had been offhand and according to Sarah downright crotchety. The two of them went into the house and we could all imagine the scene. They were both as stubborn as each other and James feared that neither would back down.

Angel had her eyes glued to the back door waiting for Binny to appear and Blackie made it quite clear he was jealous.

"Here they come!" Danny leapt up off a straw bale and tried to look busy.

"I've made a decision." Binny gave Angel a hug and tried to stroke the foal, but she was leaping around the stable like a spring lamb.

Sarah winked at Danny and I looked away when

I saw Binny's eyes welling up. She loved Angel to bits and what she said next couldn't have been easy.

"I've decided to leave Angel here for the next six months, at least until the foal is weaned." Katie's eyes tripled in size. "I've been stupid, possessive, expected too much. I don't know, it's never easy accepting that you're too old to do certain things."

"But there's still life in you yet." Trevor looked terribly earnest and Binny put a hand on his shoulder.

"I'm not on the scrap heap yet, Trevor, but I'm no match for that young thing." The foal stared at her, then swished her little tail and started chewing Katie's welly.

"I'm giving her to Hollywell Stables – you'll know what to do with her."

We all stood gaping like fish.

"You m-mean...?" Danny couldn't get his words out.

"She's ours?" Katie's voice was so high it could have broken glass.

"I think that's another way of putting it," Binny grinned.

"Our very own foal!" Katie looked as if she was going to pass out.

"For ever?" Danny was shaking his head, hardly able to take it in.

"And I've made a decision about my own life." Binny went on. "Loneliness is the worst disease of old age so I've finally agreed to marry Jimmy – the man must have the patience of a saint."

"Yippee!" Katie yelled and then half jumped out of her skin when the foal bit her bottom.

"Way to go, Mrs A." Trevor shook Binny's hand vigorously and I thought he'd never let go.

"We're going on a cruise and then of course I'll be back to see Angel. You can't get rid of me that easily."

"You've done the right thing," Sarah said.

"I think Frank would have approved," Katie added, showing oodles of maturity.

"So, as far as I can see, there's only one thing left," Binny said, "and that's, what are you going to call the foal?"

"Blossom, Brandy, Lola, Kizzy . . . or maybe Red or Saffron or what about Sabre or Honey?"

"Katie, not now, we're in the middle of a major crisis!"

We really were up the creek without a paddle as Trevor put it. People were pouring through the gates in a constant stream. There were so many families, so many cars, so many children wanting to see every single horse and pony. The Hollywell shop was doing good business and Mrs Mac had to keep sending Blake to the store room for more supplies. Everybody seemed to be walking round in Hollywell baseball caps and T-shirts.

"It's heaving," Ross shouted across a sea of bobbing heads. "We can't keep up with the teas and coffees, it's like watering the five thousand."

There was a tailback of cars right down the lane as far as the eye could see and one of the neighbours had rung up to tell us all the main roads were jam-packed and traffic was moving about ten miles an hour. People were turning out in their hundreds.

Stalls were set out in each stable and we'd even got the blacksmith giving a display of how horseshoes are made. The cake stall sold out within an hour and loads of people were walking round with bottles of home-made wine and beer. James and Mrs Mac's husband were serving people left, right and centre.

Binny had miraculously set us up with a burger bar at the very last minute, Mr Pirelli's Mobile Munchies, and the smell of tomato ketchup and sizzling sausages was wafting out around the stables. I was just making my way over to grab a burger when Sarah appeared, flushed and desperate, waving her hand in the air.

"We really are in trouble now," she said. "Rocky's just phoned on his mobile – his limousine is stuck in the traffic, it doesn't look as if he's going to make it."

Rocky was supposed to be here in the next hour to cut the red ribbon and officially open a new row of stables we'd had built. We also had everything set up for him to sing "Chase the Dream", the number one record which Rocky had dedicated to Hollywell Stables. He had to get here – without Rocky the whole thing would die a death.

"We'll have to start the parade soon," Sarah squeaked. "All we need now is the loudspeaker to go on the blink."

"Have you ever heard of something being too successful?" Blake pushed past a family with three children and a pushchair and nearly got daubed with strawberry ice-cream. "We ought to get them into the field," he said, "make more room."

"Isn't it wonderful!" Katie came up wearing a pair of huge dangly ear-rings still complete with the price tag, and Danny wandered past reeking of men's aftershave.

"What are we going to do?" Sarah almost screamed. And short of dressing Ross up in a wig and disguise I honestly didn't have a clue.

"Just go with the flow," said James.

I spent the next hour pointing out some of the ponies in the field and telling crowds of people their life stories. A year ago I would never have had the confidence to do that and now nobody could shut me up. In fact Ross said if I kept going on like that I could talk for Britain.

Everybody seemed to be having a fantastic time and still more people were piling in. I vaguely saw Mrs Mac, bright red in the face and guzzling lemonade, and Jigsaw loping off from the Punch and Judy stall with a very lop-sided Punch. The car-parks were causing a few problems and already two cars had got stuck. Even though the sun was shining it still wasn't enough to dry out the ground. Heaven knows what we were going to use to tow them out. Some of the portable loos were causing problems because the canvas sides hadn't been pegged down nearly well enough and one poor woman went scarlet when a gust of wind caught her unawares.

"Mel, where's Sarah? We're all ready for the parade." Trevor tried to fight off a horde of kids with a water pistol.

"Now we'll have none of that round the horses," I said. I could do with a badge marked "Official".

Blake fetched me an ice-cream and said I'd

127

earned a rest, and we nipped into the house for a ten-minute breather.

"It's incredible out there," he said, drinking some water from the cold water tap.

I bumped into a chair and then realized I was still wearing my sunglasses, which was why everything was so dark.

"Mel, will you stand still for a minute and listen to me. I tried to tell you the other night. I'm not going to Ireland. I've found Tina somebody else. I'm staying right here with you and the horses."

My jaw moved up and down a couple of times but nothing came out and I was still squinting, trying to adjust to the light.

"If you keep holding your head down you'll get a double chin," Blake laughed.

"I could murder you, Blake Kildaire. Have you any idea what you've put me through?"

Suddenly the loudspeaker burst into life and we could hear Sarah's voice and then some music.

"Come on." Blake grabbed my hand. "We'll miss the parade."

Everybody was moving out of the yard into the roped-off ring where Katie and Danny were hanging on to Queenie and Bluey and the rest of the helpers were trying to do their best with the other horses.

"Walter's eaten the flower display and someone's

hat." Ross came up carrying a straw hat with no rim. "And somebody's been feeding Isabella cheeseburgers and now she won't move."

"It doesn't matter." I gave him a cheesy grin. "Everything's just perfect."

"And the first pony to lead the parade is Queenie, our lucky mascot." Sarah did the commentary from the Pony Club caravan. Then came Bluey, Colorado, Terence and Dancer. Sarah gave each one a case history and progress report and they were trotted round the ring to a round of applause. James had somehow found a camcorder and was trying to video it over someone's shoulder.

"Dancer is a pure thoroughbred, an ex-race-horse who we found neglected in a field in the middle of winter with pneumonia." Sarah's voice was brimming with emotion and everybody was straining to hear every word. It was wonderful.

A lot of the crowd were members of the fan club with badges and knew each horse and pony by name. One young girl had knitted a patchwork quilt for Queenie but she'd got carried away and it was a size more suitable for Big Boris.

"Never mind, dear, you can do another one for next year."

"I don't think I can take this in." Blake looked up at the powder-blue sky, one hand shading his eyes. "Do tell me I'm seeing things."

Everybody had suddenly fallen quiet and was looking up at the sky.

"This is just so typical." Sarah came out of the caravan and nearly fell down with shock.

A huge bright-red balloon was hovering over Hollywell with two people in the basket, one of whom we recognized immediately. He was waving like mad and trying to shout something but we couldn't hear.

"It's Rocky!" a big burly man yelled out from behind Blake.

"Good Lord, he's right," someone else piped up.

"What an entrance!" A chorus of voices struck up. "Rocky!" Everybody thought it was part of the show.

Rocky stepped out of the hot-air balloon, as athletic as a teenager and oozing star quality. He swept across the grass, his long dark hair rippling down his back and his white streak glinting in the sunshine.

"Rocky!" Everybody was shouting and screaming like mad and then they all remembered the horses and quietened down.

Rocky bowed as if he'd just done a stage show and then Sarah ran up and grabbed his arm and hissed, "Why didn't you tell us what you were up to?"

Apparently Rocky had got fed up sitting in the

back of the limousine and then he'd noticed a crowd of people with hot-air balloons in a huge field off the road. It was some special club and it didn't take two minutes for Rocky to explain his situation and one of them came to the rescue.

"They were fantastic," Rocky said. "I've even decided to buy one of my own."

Sarah groaned, and I suddenly had visions of Rocky popping in for afternoon tea in a big balloon and groaned too.

Rocky was whisked off to sign autographs and then he popped into the caravan to make a speech. "As patron of Hollywell Stables . . ."

"Isn't he just delicious?" A woman fanned herself with a hanky and then recognized the straw hat I was holding and gave a little sob.

Trevor, who was completely starstruck, became even more overcome when somebody drove a brand-new tractor up the Hollywell drive, decorated all over with pink toilet roll.

"Mrs Mac and I had a little chat last time I was here," Rocky explained guiltily. "I couldn't resist."

"But Rocky, a brand-new tractor." Trevor's eyes were still spinning.

Rocky wanted to know where the welly-wanging competition was, and the skittles – Mrs Mac had told him all about it – but Sarah insisted it was time for "Chase the Dream".

"Look, it's the fire brigade," Ross said, and we all recognized the burly men walking around with their families, now out of uniform.

Rocky picked up the microphone and the backing band struck up the first notes. It had taken ages to get a makeshift stage set up but it was worth it to hear Rocky sing what had become our theme song.

"I'm so happy," Danny breathed beside me and we all swayed to the music and joined in with the chorus.

When it was over Rocky cut the red ribbon and then joined Sarah in the caravan for the second half of the parade.

Boris, Jakey, little Fluffy, Walter, Sally, Snowy, Arnie, even Isabella was there – all the ponies we'd brought over from France and all the scores of others we'd rescued since we'd opened the Hollywell gates to any waif or stray.

"Look." Blake held my hand as Blackie gingerly walked alongside Danny to finish off the parade. Angel was ahead of him with the foal and Blackie never took his eyes off either of them.

"Danny calls him Superdad," Blake grinned. "Can you believe the difference?"

I rammed my sunglasses on quickly because there were tears streaking down my cheeks.

"This is the best day out I've ever had." I overheard an old lady talking to Ross and happily munching away on a bag of home-made fudge.

"Mel, Mel!" Katie came tearing along like a sprint runner after leaving Angel with Binny. She was gasping for breath when she finally reached me.

"Mel, I've thought of a name for the foal, and Binny agrees and Sarah—"

"Whoa, whoa, one thing at a time. What's the name?"

Katie gasped a couple more times and then grinned from ear to ear.

"Holly," she said, "after Hollywell Stables. What do you think?"

What could I think? It was perfect. The best.

"And we could call her Hollywell Daydream for her show name." And then she raced off again because she said Holly would be missing her.

Rocky went back on to the makeshift stage to give another burst of "Chase the Dream", and we all stood and cheered until we were hoarse.

Hollywell Stables was a success story . . . and I'd never felt more proud in my whole life.

Hollywell Stables 1

Flying Start by Samantha Alexander

Hollywell Stables – sanctuary for horses and ponies. It was a dream come true for Mel, Ross and Katie . . .

A mysterious note led them to Queenie, neglected and desperately hungry, imprisoned in a scrap-yard. Rescuing Colorado was much more complicated. The spirited Mustang terrified his wealthy owner: her solution was to have him destroyed.

But for every lucky horse at the sanctuary there are so many others in desperate need of rescue. And money is running out fast . . .

How can the sanctuary keep going?

Hollywell Stables 2

The Gamble by Samantha Alexander

Hollywell Stables – sanctuary for horses and ponies. It was a dream come true for Mel, Ross and Katie . . .

It was a gamble. How could it possibly work? Why should one of the world's most famous rock stars give a charity concert for Hollywell Stables? But Rocky is no ordinary star and when he discovers that the racing stables keeping his precious thoroughbred are cheating him, he leads the Hollywell team on a mission to uncover the truth . . .

Hollywell Stables 3

Revenge by Samantha Alexander

Hollywell Stables – sanctuary for horses and ponies.
It was a dream come true for Mel, Ross and Katie . . .

Emotions run high at Hollywell Stables when the local
hunt comes crashing through the yard. The consequences are disastrous, and Charles Stonehouse is to
blame.

Then one of the sanctuary's own ponies goes missing.
Could the culprit be Bazz, who is back on the scene
and out for revenge? The Hollywell team know they
have to act fast: there's no time to lose . . .

Hollywell Stables 4

Fame by Samantha Alexander

Hollywell Stables – sanctuary for horses and ponies. It was a dream come true for Mel, Ross and Katie . . .

Rocky's new record, "Chase the Dream", shoots straight into the Top Ten, and all the proceeds are going to Hollywell Stables. It brings overnight fame to the sanctuary and the family are asked to do television and radio interviews. In one show they get a call from a girl who has seen a miniature horse locked in a caravan, but rings off before telling them where it was. The Hollywell team set off to unravel the mystery . . .

Other People's Ponies
by Wendy Douthwaite

It seemed to Jess that she would never have a pony of her own. All she ever did was look after other people's ponies. First there was Beetle, then the plump and lazy Muffin, and finally there was Polly, a beautiful grey Arab mare, who was her dream pony made real. If only dreams could be made real, too!

"Polished sensitive writing about feelings and friendships which develops into an unexpected and bittersweet ending."
Books For Keeps

Polly on Location
by Wendy Douthwaite

"We think we'll need some extras, sometime next week," he explained, "some riders and ponies. It will be for a night-time scene. Smugglers coming back from the coast, some riding, some leading pack-horses, that sort of thing. And we could do with some horse help, today, too. Interested?"

When Jessica Caswell suggests to her friends in the Edgecombe Valley Riding Club that they audition for the film, she never dreamt that she and her beautiful Arab mare, Polly, would play the star roles!